STEP OF FAITH

Book 1 in the Magnolia Gardens Series

MICHELLE STIMPSON
CASANDRA MCLAUGHLIN

ALSO BY CASANDRA MCLAUGHLIN & MICHELLE STIMPSON

Not with the Church's Money

When the pastor of Lee Chapel passes away suddenly, his son, Willie Lee, Jr., is supposed to pick up the mantle. But "church" was never Willie Jr.'s forte...until his uncle Joseph convinces him that becoming the next pastor might prove beneficial financially.

Willie's mother, Ephesia, hopes that her son will be able to fill his father's shoes, but she has doubts. And Willie's aunt Galatia has no problem voicing her opinions about Willie Jr.'s deficiencies. In fact, she hopes that her husband (Joseph) will soon be able to take over the job of shepherding the church.

Amidst this uncertainty, Willie's wife decides now would be a good time to leave, which means Willie Jr. must obtain and keep a job— something he hasn't ever really had to do. Will the pressures of making ends meet cause Willie Jr. to abuse his position and the church's money? Will he ever be able to live up to the prophecy his deceased father told? And will he learn his most valuable lessons before it's too late?

The Blended Blessings Series

Book 1: A New Beginning - Sometimes love doesn't work out the first time. Or the second. Now in her third marriage, Angelia is hoping for her happily-ever-after with Darren Holley. But soon after they move into their sprawling mini-mansion, Darren's new job as a high school football coach in a championship-hungry Texas town leaves Angelia feeling like a single mother to her two children as well as Darren's twin diva-daughters. Not to mention the drama from Darren's mother, who can't get over the fact that her son has married a woman with so much baggage.

When Angelia confides in a few ladies from the local church, their nice, sweet, holy-wife advice may prove too burdensome. Should Angelia cut her losses and get out before the ink settles on their marriage certificate, or will she finally learn the true meaning of perseverance as she and Darren attempt to blend two very different backgrounds in the face of adversity *and* nosy church folk?

Book 2: *Through It All* - Angelia Holley knows she'd never win a mother-of-the-year award. But was her example so bad that it drove her daughter, Amber, to repeat the pattern of teenage pregnancy? And why did Amber pick J.D. of all people to father her baby?

While Angelia is forming a bond with her stepdaughter, Skylar, twin sister Tyler isn't nearly as fond of the new "family" forming in the Holley household. When Tyler starts to act out, will Angelia be able to keep her mouth shut and let her husband and the girls' mother work this out?

And the baby of the family, Demarcus, suddenly wants to bond with his biological father. Should Angelia swallow her pride, over look the years of lack of financial/emotional support, and allow Demarcus to form a bond with the man who has never been there for him?

Join Angelia and Darren Holley as they continue with the grow- ing pains of a blended family as they grow in their knowledge of the One who can help them through.

Book 3: Peace of Mind - Angelia Holley hopes that things in her blended family have made a turn for the better. She and her step-daughter, Tyler, are getting along better. Twin Skylar has fully recuperated from surgery and Angelia is even learning to embrace her new role as a much-too-young grandmother.

Just when Angelia gets a firm handle on life, up pops drama in the form of Javar—her oldest child's father, who had been imprisoned. Will Angelia be able to put her past life with her previous boo behind? Will Javar want a relationship with Amber and Dylan?

And then there's her meddling mother-in-law, Mother Holley. Will she ever accept Angelia as Darren's wife? Will Angelia's prayer group be able to help her stand on the word and her faith, trusting God to work it out?

Join Darren and Angelia in the final book of the Blended Blessings series to see if they will ever have peace of mind.

DEDICATION

To the "old saints" who prayed for us,
ministered to us, and labored over us
even when we didn't have sense enough to appreciate it.
We are thankful for your influence.

ACKNOWLEDGMENTS

CaSandra and Michelle wish to thank the Lord for His unfailing love and grace and the talent He has given us to share His truths through writing.

Special thanks to Paulette Nunlee, who graciously offered to edit our book in support of our upcoming movie, Deacon Brown's Daughters. We really appreciate you!

Thank you the readers who continue to support our work. We pray that the Magnolia Gardens series will be a blessing to you!

CHAPTER 1

THIS USED TO BE THE BEST DAY OF THE YEAR. FAMILY, friends, food, gifts. Sometimes even singing, if her husband's arthritic fingers allowed him to tickle the ivories through a verse of Silent Night.

The kids used to wake up before sunrise to open their gifts. And, of course, Frenchetta Davenport would barely sleep the night before. She and Elroy might have stayed up half the night, with him assembling toys and her cooking for a scrumptious breakfast and belt-busting lunch. Entertaining and making memories in their fifty-five hundred square-foot home had been the joy of Frenchetta's life.

"Frenchie, you've outdone yourself," people would remark, rubbing their stomachs. Some of them even asked to spend a few hours sleeping in the guest room before they hit the road. Of course, Frenchetta was happy to oblige their requests. People needed her hospitality, her kindness. They benefited from her cooking and housekeeping skills. For Frenchetta, there was no greater purpose in life than those kinds of days.

But this Christmas Day, none of her skills were needed. Elroy was gone. Three Christmases had passed since his sudden hearth attack.

The kids had told her it was too hard to come back home now that their father was dead. "It's just not the same," Katrina said over the phone that first year.

Keith hadn't even bothered to call until after dark. And he sounded drunk on the other end of the line. "Momma, I'll come by tomorrow."

"What are you doing now?" Frenchetta had badgered him.

"I'm at my girlfriend's house."

"Well, you can come by when you finish over there, right?"

Keith hesitated. Sniffed. "I can't. I just can't."

The first Christmas, Frenchetta had understood. The kids were devastated. The second Christmas, she'd managed to talk them into coming over for breakfast at least. She made their favorites—cranberry scones for Katrina, chocolate chip pancakes for Keith. She'd even made French toast for Katrina's twins, though they were barely old enough to chew solid food.

All that food went to waste, however, because nobody came. Nobody. Instead, they had sent text messages with lame excuses for why they weren't coming.

So, this Christmas Frenchetta didn't bother with cooking or even asking. She'd read an article in a senior magazine about letting go and letting your adult kids make decisions about how they wanted to spend their holidays. She wasn't supposed to try to manipulate or guilt-trip her kids into spending holidays with her. The article assured her that adult children were reasonable and would eventually see the value of aged wisdom in their lives and their children's lives. "It's the circle of life," the article had said. "Humans are wired for multi-generational connection."

Well, if that was true, then Frenchetta's children must be aliens. They could go weeks and months without seeing or speaking to her.

Except, of course, when they needed money. Katrina was married, but she and her husband struggled to pay their bills from time to time. And Keith... *Lord, help.* He was still chasing dreams. He'd even changed his name to LaJermaine and insisted that she refer to him by this new name—unless she was writing out a check to him.

Forget that stupid article. Frenchetta could call Keith and work her way into a conversation about his need for money. He'd come some time in the next few days.

The phone rang, sending Frenchetta's heart racing. She didn't glance at the small blue wording on the phone's console because it was Christmas Day and she wanted some sort of surprise.

Somebody loves me.

"Hello! Merry Christmas!" she answered cheerfully.

The pause should have been her first clue that something was wrong. "Hello. This is Dixon's Pharmacy calling regarding..."

Frenchetta didn't need to listen to the automated call. Tears strolled down her cheek as she pressed the number one to refill her monthly supply of her high cholesterol medication.

"Press pound to confirm your refill."

For a split moment, Frenchetta thought about not pressing the pound button. *What does it matter if I'm well or not?*

Her index finger hovered over the button for a second longer before she gave herself a quick pep talk. "Thank God you're still alive, Frenchie. Healthy, wealthy, wise."

She pushed the button, ensuring that her life-saving medication would be available for pick-up the next day.

But the whole incident scared her. She wasn't exactly suicidal; she just didn't have a huge reason to live. Nothing to look forward to. Unlike her friends who constantly posted pictures at their grandchildren's birthday parties and family vacations on social media, Frenchetta didn't have a close relationship with her adult children.

Come to think of it, she wouldn't have described her relationship with them as "close" even when they were younger. She loved them, of course, from the very beginning. *How could she not?* She and Elroy had no children for the first nine years of their marriage. Then, all of a sudden, her prayers were answered and they suddenly had two.

On top of that, she loved Elroy, and the kids were perfect little representations of their love for one another. Both had Elroy's deep brown skin and Frenchetta's "rabbit" nose. Katrina's little hands mirrored her mother's even from birth, and Keith grew into the spitting image of his father as he approached twenty. Handsome, distinguished-looking.

Elroy worked hard in city administration and business consulting, securing the family's wealth and reputation in Orchid Falls. The Davenports had been the picture-perfect well-off clan. Private schools, vacations abroad, a summer home in Virginia while the kids were growing up.

None of that mattered now. Frenchetta didn't regret putting her kids in all those extracurricular activities or making them participate in the cotillions and the talent competitions. That's what every black family who could afford it did for their kids. They were trying to catch up for generations of setbacks and oppression. Education was the great equalizer, and it was important to project an image that proclaimed, "We are just as good as anyone else."

But Frenchetta wondered now, sitting alone in the lavish decor of her custom-built home, if it had been worth it all. Pushing the kids to perfection, keeping up with the Joneses, teaching them the "importance" of appearing in control at all times. "Never let people see you sweat. That'll make them think you're weak."

Maybe she should have let them sweat. And cry. And be imperfect, even while black. Maybe, then, they would have had some kind of feelings about her. Maybe they would have cared enough to come see about their lonely sixty-year-old mother on Christmas Day.

Frenchetta unbraided her single braid and tussled her long, graying brown hair. This wavy hair had been her signature for as long as she could remember. The full mane was a perfect complement to her small frame, which had made her one of Elroy's greatest prides.

A lot of good my looks are doing me now.

The phone rang again. This time, Frenchetta checked to see who was calling, so as not to get her hopes up.

The caller ID showed 'Gloria Young,' Frenchetta's friend from her days at Hopewell Church.

"Hey, Frenchie! Merry Christmas!"

Frenchetta could hear the rumble of Gloria's family members in the background. "Hey, Glo. Merry Christmas to you, too."

"You all right, Frenchie?"

Frenchetta winced. She hadn't done a very good job of following her own advice because, obviously, Glo had picked up on the distress. "Well, you know. Another Christmas without the kids or my grandkids."

"Where is everybody?"

"Who knows? They haven't called."

"It's only one o'clock. Maybe they'll get in touch later." Gloria suggested.

"I ain't holding my breath." Frenchetta sighed.

"Why don't you come on over here with us," Gloria said. "We've got plenty of food."

"Oh no. I don't want to intrude," Frenchetta declined.

"You're not intruding, I'm inviting you," Gloria said. "In fact, I insist."

"You insist?" Frenchetta laughed. "Girl, you are funny."

"I'm serious, Frenchie. You and I are barely sixty years old. It ain't time to pack up yet. Come on over. Jake made those cookies you like, and I think we're going to go over to see Emma and Paul later. Their senior living place is having an 80s Christmas dance tonight—can you believe that?"

"Oh wow," Frenchetta remarked. "I guess they're living it up in there, huh?"

"I told you. If it were up to me, I'd be there in a heartbeat. But you know Jake. He wants a place to call his own."

"Yeah."

"But there's nothing holding *you* back from moving to one of those places," Gloria added. "Might do you some good. I know you'd have a blast at the Christmas dance!"

For the first time, Frenchetta seriously considered Gloria's words. Like Jake, she'd always had her sights set on owning a piece of America. But today—when that piece seemed so lonely—what was it worth?

"You coming over, girl?"

Frenchetta stood and examined her pale reflection in the mirror. *Good Lord, I need some sunlight.* "Yeah, I guess so."

"That's my Frenchie. You've got a lot of life left to live, girl!"

Frenchetta smiled, thinking Gloria had no idea how timely her statement was.

CHAPTER 2

THREE MONTHS LATER

FRENCHETTA COULDN'T BELIEVE HOW QUICKLY HER HOUSE had sold. Margaret Humprey of Humprey Real Estate had placed the house on the market and in two weeks she had a buyer. She'd promised Frenchetta a quick sale, and she got more than she'd expected. After all Orchid Falls was a well to do neighborhood, and most of the houses there were older which meant more land for homeowners. None of the houses were close together like most neighborhoods. When the Lawrence family came to view the house Frenchetta had hoped they'd be the ones to get the house.

"Honey, this is it. This is the home I want," Nancy Lawrence exclaimed!

"Well, if you're sure, then let's close the deal," he proudly said.

Frenchetta admired how Nancy looked at her husband Ralph. They reminded her so much of how she and Elroy had been when they were courting. She'd watched them share stares and make googly eyes at one another as they oohed and aahed in every room. Oh how she missed those days.

We've shared some great memories in this house. It's time to make some new ones

Frenchetta continued to put the last of her things in her Lexus SUV, took one final look at the house and made her way to Magnolia Gardens.

Magnolia Gardens was an upscale Senior Retirement Living Complex. It was luxury at its finest. Everything you needed was under one roof. There was a salon, cafeteria, fitness center, recreational center, sauna, pool area, laundry room, ice cream parlor, movie theatre, library, a chapel, and they had licensed professional care available twenty-four hours a day for those in need of care. They offered a plethora of amenities and weekly activities. Tuscan decor, fountains and fireplaces were on the patio. It was truly a Tuscan villa with the luxury of concierge services and the security of a gated community.

After attending the Christmas party with Glo, Frenchetta had made up her mind that Magnolia Gardens would be her new home. She'd paid her deposit and did the necessary paperwork to move into a King Deluxe Suite which consisted of a bedroom, closet, living room, bathroom, and kitchenette.

"Welcome to Magnolia Gardens," the gate attendant greeted Frenchetta as she gave him her code to gain access to enter.

"Morning." She smiled as she waited for him to scan her card.

"Alright Ms. Davenport, if you'd follow the sign that says garage, Milton our parking attendant will show you your private garage.

Frenchetta thanked him and followed the sign. She'd requested a room on the first level and they'd obliged and also gave her a room closest to the garage exit.

Frenchetta pulled into her assigned spot, popped the truck and got out to retrieve her things.

"Need some help," a chubby, slightly-bald man said.

"Ah, yeah sure." Frenchetta checked out his tacky apparel that consisted of a wrinkled shirt and a pair of pajama bottoms as she handed him her suitcase.

"I'm Zeke Hudson." He smiled.

"I'm Frenchetta Davenport, but my friends call me Frenchie." She gave him a warm friendly smile.

"Glad to make your acquaintance. What floor are you taking your things to?"

"Oh I'm on the first floor, room 1081."

"Do you have your key?"

"Oh yeah, it's in my purse." She unzipped the red Coach bag she'd purchased for herself as a Christmas gift.

Frenchetta opened the door, and Zeke followed suit and placed the suitcase in the living room.

"I'll let you get settled." He turned to leave.

"Thanks again." She extended her hand and shook his.

After Zeke left, Frenchetta closed the door and unpacked her clothes. Although she could smell Pine-Sol, she still wanted to clean before placing her toiletries in the bathroom.

She sat aside the king size bed thinking of Katrina and Keith. Neither of them knew she'd moved, and she hadn't bothered to tell them.

They'll probably find out I moved when I die.

A light tap on the door disturbed her thoughts.

She opened the door, and to her surprise, a pale-skinned, orange-red haired, freckle faced lady dressed in way too many colors for Frenchetta's liking stood at the door with a crocheted mat that said "Home" on it.

"Hello, I'm Lily. I'm your neighbor. Welcome to Magnolia Gardens." She smiled, showing that she had several teeth missing.

"I'm Frenchetta, but you can call me Frenchie."

"That's like Frenchie from Grease, like French's mustard, like French fries, well not really. But that's different." She laughed.

"I like the term unique instead." Frenchie pointed out.

"This is for you." Lily handed her the mat.

"Why, thank you," Frenchetta said.

"Well, I gotta get going. My hair appointment is in a few minutes." Lily ran her fingers through her hair.

"Nice meeting you. I'm sure I'll be seeing plenty of you." Frenchetta closed the door.

That poor thing is stuck in the 70s.

The sound of her phone ringing caught her off guard. The ring tone revealed that it was Keith calling. She'd assigned "For The Love of Money" by the O'Jays as his ring tone because that's the only time he called.

"Momma, why you sell the house?" Keith said, getting right to the point before she could even say hello.

"I'm fine, Keith, how are you?"

"I was fine 'til I drove to the house and found out that my key don't work no more. And please stop calling me Keith. My name is LaJermaine."

"Your name is Keith, not LaJermaine. You need to grow up and wake up, and realize that part of your life is over."

Keith was in a rap group in the 90s called La-La-La. They were trying to put all of their names together like some of the other groups back in the day. La Derrick and LaJordan had told him that LaKeith didn't make sense, so he chose to be LaJermaine. They actually won a contest at the mall singing their hit song, "Your Love Put Me In A Coma." Keith was still waiting to be signed by some big record company, and since they still sung at birthday parties from time to time, he believed they'd one day be famous.

"Daddy left the house for us, not just you," he snapped.

"I beg your pardon. You've lost your mind. The house belongs to me, and why do you care anyway? You don't come to the house unless you want something." She choked back her tears.

"Well can I come by to get my portion of the money?"

"Your portion of *what* money?"

"From the house. I know you got a good chunk of cash."

"You really are a piece of work. I'm not giving you a dime. You had your money from your father's insurance, and you blew it on foolishness. And you think it's an AFM over here."

"It's a ATM, Momma. Why you gotta try to be funny?" He laughed.

"Oh, this isn't a joke. I know exactly what I'm saying. You

think everything is Automatically Frenchetta's Money," she said matter-of-factly.

"Oh, now since you living in foo-foo-she-she-land, high on the hog, now you don't wanna help your only son out."

"Who told you where I live?"

"You know Ms. Glo is like an old refrigerator; she can't hold nothing. But, that's besides the point. I'll be by there tomorrow so that we can discuss this. Daddy wouldn't want you to sell the house, nor would he want you to leave me and Katrina out."

"You don't know what your father—"

Keith had hung up the phone before she could finish her statement.

I dare he call me with his so-called demands. Maybe I should have asked him and Katrina. But for what? They don't really care. Just selfish.

Another knock at the door startled her from her thoughts.

She at first started not to answer, because her mood had turned sour. But, whoever was on he other side of the door was persistent.

Frenchetta opened the door and was greeted by a very attractive man.

"Hello, I'm Norman Walker, and I'm one of the resident directors."

"I'm Frenchetta Davenport. All of my friends call me Frenchie." She batted her eyes.

"I heard some shouting. Is everything okay?"

Frenchetta couldn't help but check him out. He reminded her of a darker version of Billy Dee Williams. His skin was smooth, baring no moles or scars. Just a few wrinkles in his forehead. His hair was semi curly with a salt and pepper blend, and so was his facial hair. She loved his outfit of jeans, flannel grey and black shirt, and a black fedora hat.

"It will be. That was just my son. You know how kids can be," she said, sounding like a damsel in distress.

"I can relate. I have two of my own." He smiled, showing off his deep dimples. "How'd you like to join us for Bingo? That'll help get your mind off of your son."

"I haven't played Bingo in years." She giggled.

"Well, I'm sure you'll have fun. We start in anhour in Dulaney Hall. Hope to see you there."

"Okay thanks, Norman." She watched him walk away.

Hmmph, maybe moving here was the best decision after all.

CHAPTER 3

Keith couldn't believe his eyes as he neared Monica's apartment building. There, on the concrete leading to the staircase to her rented space were his belongings. Several pairs of shoes, jeans, shirts, his video game console as well as a stack of video games. His signature red, yellow, and green leather Jamaican jacket removed any doubt the items belonged to him.

"What the—"

"Man, that's your stuff?" the Uber driver asked.

"Yeah. I...What in the world?"

"I don't know what you did, but somebody's mad at you," the driver said with a slight chuckle.

Keith didn't justify the comment. He hopped out of the car and ran over to the pile. He yelled up to the window of Monica's kitchen. "Monica!"

She opened it and hollered, "Leave, LaJermaine, or I'll call the police!"

"What's wrong with you? Why is all my stuff out here?"

Monica was not one to resort to such dramatic antics. In all the six years he had known her, she was the biggest pushover. She was always available to him. Things only got more convenient when she gave birth to their son, Keith, Jr., six years ago. No black woman wants to be left alone to raise a son in American society, and Keith took full advantage of this fact. All he had to say was, "But I want to be here for my son," and Monica would melt, give in, change her mind, and give him another chance.

Today was certainly a good day to play the Daddy-card. "What about our son, Monica? Don't you want me in his life?"

"Not if you're going to set a bad example."

Despite the emotion in her voice, Keith had to admit himself that this was a new one from Monica. She'd never despised him so much that it mattered more than their son. Until today. He had to try a new tactic.

"Monica, what about all this time we done put into our relationship? You want to just throw it all away?"

The man in the apartment below theirs, who often had to beat on the ceiling to get Keith and Monica to stop arguing so loudly, yelled out, "Shut up and go see a counselor!" from behind his closed window.

Keith shook his head. His father would have called this a "ghetto moment," two people airing their business in front of an entire complex.

Keith grabbed his favorite Jordans and headed upstairs. He bammed on the door repeatedly. "Monica. Come on! I love you and KJ. You have to let me back in. I'm sorry." He didn't even know exactly what he'd done, but whatever reason

Monica had, he knew was valid. Could have been another woman, another broken promise, another lie. He was guilty of all the above.

"LaJermaine," Monica said resolutely from the other side of the door, "I am done. I am tired. I can't do this anymore. Go away. You are not on my lease. You don't pay any bills here. If I call the police right now, I'll be able to successfully get a restraining order against you. Just leave."

He knocked on the door one last time. "What did I do?"

"What didn't you do? And why didn't you pay the water bill?"

Water wasn't the real problem, though. He had been promising to pay bills since they met, but he'd never actually done so on a regular basis. But Monica hadn't kicked him out before now.

Suddenly, he knew what the problem was. Monica had started going to church. And reading books by all those women empowerment people. They were filling her head with all the ideas about wanting more, being more, self-esteem, and all that stuff women tell each other to make them hate men.

He had one more trick up his sleeves. The age-old phrase that had saved relationships since the beginning of time. "Monica, I love you."

"I wish you did, LaJermaine. I really do. But the truth is, you only love yourself. And since you ain't gonna love me, it's time for me to start loving me. Now leave."

He was certain now that Monica had listened to one too many podcasts. Her tone, her words, and the strength behind them wasn't the Monica he had known all these years.

Keith knew women. He knew when they were fed up with

him. For once, he actually did care about what this might mean for their son. "What are we going to do about KJ?

"We'll have the courts arrange visitation after I file for child support."

Those last two words nearly made Keith see double vision. "Child support?"

"Yes. Child support. And I'm moving, so don't try to come back here and start trouble. You'll get all the documents you need from the judge. I'm going to count to five now, and you'd better be gone or I'm calling the police. One."

"Monica. You for real?"

"Two."

"Monica!" He slapped an open fist against the door.

"Three!"

After a few cuss words, Keith thought it best to leave the premises. He didn't have a record, and today wouldn't be a good day to get one. Especially now that his main safety net, his mother, was acting funny. She might not bail him out.

"Females trippin!" He quickly descended the staircase and loaded his belongings into his non-working Ford Escape. The SUV's paint and body looked like a perfectly fine car, but he'd blown the engine by failing to change the oil. He needed money from Frenchetta to get back on his feet. His parents' home had always been available when he was between women. Until now.

"Somebody's gotta help me," he said under his breath, heaving a third load of clothing into the vehicle. His mind raced as he tried to think of his next prospect. He had a lot of female friends, but which one would let him move in *today*?

Maybe Iesha, his second child's mother. It was near the

first of the month, so she'd still have some money. Enough to support him until he either got Monica back in check or found a job and got an apartment of his own. He could stay there for at least three months before the eviction process was complete.

After he finished loading the SUV, Keith jumped into the driver's seat and called Iesha.

She didn't answer, so he sent her a text. *Miss you, baby. Can we try again? At least for Brittney's sake?*

A few minutes later, Iesha texted back. *At work. Call you tomorrow.*

"Tomorrow!" Keith yelled at the phone. "And what is she doing with a job?" Iesha had never worked. She was probably messing up her benefits by getting a job. No free food at her house.

What's gotten into these broads lately? First, Monica got all empowered, and now Iesha has a J-O-B that she couldn't even step away from to make a phone call?

Keith punched his steering wheel.

The only person left on his list who wouldn't take at least a few days of romancing before moving in was Shay. She was, maybe, the mother of his third child. DNA tests hadn't confirmed it, and Shay wasn't pushing the issue, so he wasn't going to ask any questions. He was fine with having two-and-a-possible.

If only his mother hadn't sold the house, he wouldn't be sitting there in a good-for-nothing car with all his stuff in the back and nowhere to go.

She had no right to sell that house! How could she? That was selfish of her. It was all her fault that Keith was now officially homeless. *Well, since she made the problem, she should fix it.*

Keith googled the name of the facility Glo had mentioned. Magnolia Gardens. The address popped up readily. He tapped the app for another Uber and waited for the ride with as many of his things as he could fit in his arms and a backpack. His mother was not going to ruin his life and then run away.

WHEN KEITH ARRIVED AT MAGNOLIA GARDENS, HIS BLOOD boiled over the top. The place might as well have been Caesars Palace. All the rich, old folks just chilling. Relaxing. Doing nothing at all. To the right, he saw a cafeteria. Down the hallway, he saw signs above several openings: Coffee shop and Theater.

Theater! Why do old people need a theater when all they do is sleep all day?

Keith shook his head. His mother had to be out of her mind moving to a place like this. He could only imagine how much money she was wasting at Magnolia Gardens. Money his father had worked hard to earn. Money that should have been his, too.

Keith readjusted the weight of his backpack as he approached the receptionist's desk. "Hi. I'm looking for Frenchetta Davenport. I'm her son."

"Oh, wonderful," the elderly lady sang.

Her cheerful voice irritated Keith. All these happy people and he was so miserable.

"I'll give her a call."

Keith waited on one of the plush couches. That couch

probably cost more than everything he owned. His foot tapped thinking about how his life had gone downhill while his mom was apparently "coming up."

"Hey, Keith!"

"LaJermaine!" he said forcefully. "Momma! What are you doing here?"

His mother's smile slipped away and her hands, which had been prepared for a hug, dropped to her sides. "Well, I was thinking it was good to see you, but I don't know now."

Keith motioned at the lavishly decorated lobby. "What is all this? You've moved into the Greenleaf Mansion with Daddy's money?" he said, referring to the popular TV show on the OWN network.

"Daddy's money is my money, too. I supported him through all his career and I sacrificed my life—"

"But *you* didn't work." Keith pointed at her. "And now you got all this?"

"Yes, I do. That's how it is, Keith. When a spouse sacrifices and keeps the family going while the other one works, the retirement belongs to both of them. Your father couldn't have worked sixty something-odd hours a week if I hadn't been home raising you and your sister. Making his lunches every day, getting his clothes ready, making sure you two were taken care of. It takes two to raise a family, you know."

"But I'm his *son!*"

His mother crossed her arms and shifted her weight to one side. "And what did *you* do to support your father?"

"I was born!"

MICHELLE STIMPSON & CASANDRA MCLAUGHLIN

She laughed. "And you think because you were *born* you're owed something, Keith?"

"I told you, my name—"

"I ain't calling you by that stupid name! I gave birth to you, and I'm gonna call you what I called you at the hospital— Keith Anthony Davenport. Now, you listen to me. I—"

"I don't have to listen to you." Keith cut her off. "All I know is, my father's house is gone and it's your fault, and I'm gonna stay here with you in this on-land cruise ship." Keith sat on the couch again.

"Boy, you can't stay here. You gotta be fifty-five."

He shook his head. "Well, they're going to have to make an exception because I'm here to stay."

"I don't make the rules here. And neither do you. For once, you're going to have to stand on your own two feet, Keith. The end of your gravy train is now."

An old man with some mismatched clothes walked into the vicinity. "Is everything all right, Frenchie?"

CHAPTER 4

"FRENCHIE, IS THIS MAN BOTHERING YOU?" ZEKE ASKED.

"Man, stay out of this. This between me and my momma," Keith said.

"Zeke, everything is fine. Just having a discussion with my son. He's leaving soon," Frenchetta responded.

"Okay, just making sure. We don't want no trouble."

"Man, ain't no trouble. Just go on back over there and finish reading your little fishing magazine," Keith said.

Zeke stared Keith down and then nodded his head at Frenchetta, letting her know he had her back.

Frenchetta felt her face turning warm. She couldn't wait for Zeke to go to the opposite side of the room so she could give Keith a piece of her mind.

"I didn't raise you to be rude and disrespectful. How dare you come in her causing problems before I can get settled in good," she spat.

"Momma, didn't nobody tell Grady from *Sanford & Son* to interfere in our family business." He laughed.

Frenchetta couldn't help but laugh because Zeke did favor Grady just a little bit; Zeke was just larger than him.

"That's beside the point, Keith. You still know better."

"Momma, on the real, though, I need to stay here a few days 'cause Monica tripping, my car broke down, and I spent all my money to come out here. I had to catch a Uber."

"Keith, I told you that you can't stay here. This is a senior facility."

"You can sneak and let me stay for at least tonight. What I'ma do? Where I'ma go?"

"I can't sneak and let you do *nothing*. I'll get put out."

"Well at least we'll be together, and I'll have transportation." He smiled.

"Listen at you. Your whole conversation is about how you will be. Well, son, this is where I draw the line. After today I'm done with bailing you out. I'm going to go to the ATM and get just enough money for you to get out of here, and what you do after you leave won't be any of my concern." Frenchetta stood and left.

Keith watched Frenchetta walk down the hall. He needed whatever money she was willing to give him to make his way over to one of his baby mama's house. And if that didn't work, he could at least get a hotel room. Calling his sister, Katrina, wasn't an option. He knew Jonathan wouldn't let him stay because they'd gotten into a big blow up over Keith's last business idea, Gangsta Dogs.

"Man, we taking hot dogs to a whole 'notha level," he'd said.

"Alright. I'll give you five thousand dollars to get the ball rolling, but I need my money back," Jonathan told him.

Keith found a small dive in the hood and opened Gangsta Dogs. He had hot dogs and corn dogs with hot sauce, green peppers, picante sauce, and on Fridays his special was loaded fries with Great Value hamburger helper. The business lasted for about three months. Keith never paid Jonathan his money back.

"Keith, I want you to call Uber and be on your way." Frenchetta shoved two hundred dollars into his hands.

"Momma, how you gone just give me two hundred dollars? It cost me almost one hundred to come way out here to no-man's-land," he whined.

"Well that's not my issue. I didn't ask you to come, but I am asking you to leave. Now goodbye." She walked away.

"Man, that's cold. Alright, then bet. One day you'll need me and guess what? I'ma be there. You know why? 'Cause that's what family do," he yelled after Frenchetta, but she kept walking.

Keith made his Uber reservation for Shay's house, almost certain that she'd let him come stay. But, if not, he'd go to Uncle Moody's. He lived about four blocks from Shay. Uber told him it would be another twenty minutes before someone could pick him up.

Man I'm starving like Marvin. Stomach growling like a bear.

He followed the arrow that pointed towards the cafeteria. The cafeteria was set up like a little cafe. The tables were antique, with floral tops, and the interior of the cafeteria was warm and cheery, with beautiful floral wallpaper.

This is Bougeville, for real. Keith laughed.

He made his way to the counter and glanced over the menu.

"May I take your order?" asked a beautiful lady with dark chocolate skin, a dip in her chin, and long flowing braids.

"Yeah, ummm let me get a cheeseburger." Keith smiled.

"We don't have cheeseburgers," she replied with a deep accent.

"I should have known that Ummm... how you say your name?"

"It's Unoma," she pronounced it slowly.

"I'm LaJermaine. How about I call you Uno cause you could be my number one girl," he flirted.

"So what would you like, sir?" she asked, totally ignoring the fact he was flirting with her.

"Give me a chicken salad sandwich, but I don't want no croissant. Can you put it on light bread?"

"You mean wheat bread?" she asked.

"Naw light bread, white bread, Wonder Bread. You know what I mean," he explained.

"You're funny." She laughed. "Will this be cash or room charge?"

"Room charge. Charge it to Frenchetta Davenport. That's my mother." *Ain't no sense in me spending money when I don't have to.*

"Okay, your order will be ready in a few minutes."

"Thanks, milk chocolate." He grinned.

Keith found a table and called Shay; he hoped she'd let him stay. He'd play the faithful I'm so into you role to keep from being homeless, if need be.

On the second ring, she answered. "Heeeeey baby, what's going on?"

"Just thinking about you and Justin," he lied. Keith never really believed Justin was his son, but since he was the only father he knew, he rolled with it.

"Awwww, you know I'm always thinking about you. Why don't you come over?"

"I'll see. I'll holla back at you in a few minutes," he said and hung up.

Keith had no intentions of telling her he had no place to stay. Shay had been after him, asking him to commit to her ever since they met. She was a huge fan of La La La when they first started performing. Shay and her friends attended every club appearance, and she let it be known that she was willing to do any and everything just to be with LaJermaine. He, of course, took her up on her offer, but after a while he got tired of her, and she turned into a stalker. Shay knew his every move. When La La La fell hard on their luck, and when Gangsta Dogs business went down the tubes, it was Shay who gave him money for gas, food, or whatever he needed. She was his "go to" girl.

A waitress brought Keith his sandwich on wheat bread, but he didn't complain. He wolfed it down in almost two bites.

He went back to the register and waited for Unoma to finish taking care of her customer.

"I know you don't know me, but I'd like to get to know you, Uno. May I have your phone number?"

"I don't think that my boyfriend would like that," she replied.

"Well, what he don't know won't hurt him." Keith laughed.

"I would know, and I don't have any intentions on hurting him." Unoma went into the kitchen.

Keith's phone buzzed that his Uber driver was out front. He threw his trash into the waste can, grabbed his stuff, and headed out. It was time for him to head to Shay's house and play happy family with her and Justin until he could get back on his feet and beg Monica to take him back.

CHAPTER 5

FRENCHETTA'S HEAD WAS POUNDING FROM THE ENCOUNTER with Keith. She whispered under her breath, "Gonna make my blood pressure go sky-high."

"Don't let that happen," a male voice said, causing her to whip her head around to see who was walking so closely to hear her private thoughts.

Zeke stepped back and held his hands near his chest. "I'm sorry. Didn't mean to intrude."

"Well, you kind of did," Frenchetta said. It wasn't like her to be rude, but she wasn't in the mood for these friendly folk of Magnolia Gardens at the moment.

"I'm sorry. I just wanted to let you know you're doing the right thing. With your son, I mean."

Frenchetta huffed and put a hand on her hip. "Zeke, how would you know?"

He wagged his head. "Because I have kids, too. Most of us in here do, and some of the kids get to acting up when we move in these fancy, expensive places. It's like they see their inheritance flying out the window." He flapped his arms like a bird's wings.

Frenchetta's frown broke into a smirk. Maybe Zeke did understand after all.

He motioned for her to have a seat on a nearby couch.

Disarmed by his humor, she did, and he joined her.

"Why are our kids so hard-headed and entitled?" she asked.

"Oh, a lot of reasons. If you're like me, you grew up in the segregated south. Didn't have much. Had to scrimp and scrape for everything you had. You watched your parents work hard so you could have a little. And by the time you were an adult, in the 80s, some things had changed. You had more than all you had ever dreamed. The sky was the limit." Zeke pointed toward the ceiling. "Am I right so far?"

Frenchie nodded.

"So when you had your kids, you didn't want them to suffer. You didn't want them to experience hard, hopeless times. You gave them everything they needed and most of what they wanted. Still right?"

"To a tee. But you still haven't told me why they're so hard-headed and spoiled." Frenchie folded her arms and glared.

"Giving our kids everything robbed them of what it takes to make it in this world. You need grit. Perseverance. Some disappointments. You need the ability to take a lickin' and keep on tickin', and the only way you get that is to fall down, so you can get back up again."

"Huh."

"But it's never too late. Today, you gave your son an

opportunity to grow. You should be proud of yourself." Zeke smiled.

Frenchie returned his smile.

"Hey now!" a booming voice came from Frenchie's right. She turned to see a tall, slender man coming out of his room. He slammed his door shut. "Zeke, watch out there now! You can't be out her pushin' up on my new friend."

"Excuse me? I've never even met you," Frenchetta said.

"Name's Buddy." He shuffled his way to the couch. "This man tryna mess with you?"

No, but you are.

"We were just talking about kids," Zeke said. "How's your son, by the way, Buddy?"

"He's fine. Just retired from the military. But you ain't slick, Zeke. Don't try to change the subject. Are you trying to get this fine lady to spend an evening in your room, or what?"

Frenchie's neck rolled back. "I beg your pardon."

"Zeke tries to get all the women when they come to Magnolia Gardens," Buddy explained.

"I think you're talking about yourself," Zeke said. "Frenchie and I are just having a normal conversation about raising children. You're the one who came over here trying to make things messy."

"I'ma make a mess of you if you keep stepping on my territory!" Buddy shook his fist at Zeke.

Zeke stood, and suddenly the whole thing seemed comical because Zeke had to be at least a foot taller than Buddy. Buddy's rickety-looking frame was not nearly up to a scuffle with Zeke's more muscular build.

"I'm getting out of here." Frenchie stood. "You two can

duke it out if you want to. And by the way, I'm nobody's territory!"

Once back in her room, Frenchetta had to laugh. *I guess I've still got it.*

It had been a long time since two men fought over her. The last time she remembered was when Deacon Lassaire at the church was trying to pursue her and Elroy found out. Frenchetta hadn't told her husband because, honestly, if she told him every time a man made an advance at her, she'd have been telling him something every other day. Her looks had always gotten her unwelcomed double-takes and flirtatious comments. She'd even complained to a store manager once when the shoe salesman caressed her foot inappropriately.

But the incident with Deacon Lassaire was classic. In the middle of the pastor's sermon, he had sent a note to her through a church usher. The usher, however, gave the note to Brother Davenport instead of Sister Davenport. To this day, Frenchetta thought the "mistake" had been made on purpose.

Anyhow, when her husband, who had been sitting in the audience while Frenchetta was in the choir stand, got the note, he stood up immediately, walked over to the Deacon's bench and grabbed Deacon Lassaire by the suit collar.

The entire church was caught off guard, the sermon interrupted. It was like that scene in *The Color Purple* when Shug started singing and everything stopped to see what was going on with her. Only this time, everybody stopped and went outside—starting with the pastor—who was trying to break things up.

Frenchetta had run out, too, because Elroy was no match for Deacon Lassaire. He wasn't a match for anyone, actually, seeing as he probably hadn't had a fight since he was in grade school twenty years earlier.

Oh, but that day Frenchetta wasn't so sure. Her husband pushed Deacon Lassaire out into the street yelling, "I don't wanna kick your behind on the church grounds."

Cars stopped as the men argued, the notebook paper still in Elroy's hand. "Whatchu doin' sending messages like this to my wife?"

"Hey! She's a grown woman! She got a right to make up her own mind about who she wanna be with!"

Frenchetta clutched her invisible pearls as members of the congregation oohed and aahed and shook their heads. They might as well have been eight-year-olds on a playground.

"Gentlemen! Come back inside the sanctuary," Pastor demanded. "You're making a mockery of the church!"

Thinking about it now, Frenchetta was so glad they didn't have cell phones with video cameras back then because that confrontation certainly would have gone all over the world on that Youvision...YouTube...whatever they called it.

What happened between her husband and Deacon Lassaire wasn't exactly a fight, now that she was thinking about it. Her husband swung at the man a few times and basically chased him away.

For weeks, the incident was the talk of the church and the town. People who had no connection to them, whatsoever, were conjecturing things about Frenchetta, saying she must have been cheating for her husband to get so angry. "Women will do that, you know," she had overheard the gossip about herself at the beauty shop.

Frenchetta hadn't said a thing when she heard those nasty

accusations. It really wasn't her MO to address ignorant comments. She wouldn't lower herself to those women's mindsets. This ability to disconnect herself from her emotions had come in quite handy over the years. It protected her from hurt. Pain. Disappointment. She'd never had to use the disconnection with Elroy, because she never doubted that he had her best interests at heart.

But these kids were another story.

Frenchetta kicked off her Sketchers shoes and turned on the television. Between Keith, Buddy, and Zeke, Frenchetta had had more direct drama in one day than a whole year.

But Zeke said she was right to address things differently with Keith. Yes, it brought drama and a confrontation, but at least she wouldn't be letting him run over her. It helped that Magnolia Gardens had strict rules about overnight guests. She didn't have the option to give in to Keith's sob stories anymore.

Come to think of it, she rather liked the idea of not letting anyone run over her.

Yeah. I like that idea.

Another knock at the door brought a sigh from Frenchetta's lips. "Who is it?"

This had better not be Buddy.

"It's Norman."

Norman!

Frenchetta rushed to the door. "Hello, Norman. How can I help you?"

"Wanted to run that Bingo offer by you again."

"Most definitely," Frenchetta said without hesitation.

"Excellent. You'll be my special guest."

CHAPTER 6

"Norman, give me a minute and I'll be ready. Would you like to come in?" Frenchetta asked.

Norman followed her inside and took a seat on the couch. "Take your time, I'll wait for you."

Frenchetta rushed over to the couch and put her shoes on, grabbed her purse, and went into the bathroom. She rummaged through her makeup bag and found her rose-colored lipstick she'd gotten as a sample and then put some powder on her nose. Satisfied with her look, she winked at herself in the mirror, took a deep breath, and walked back into the living room.

"I hope I didn't keep you waiting too long, Norman," she said in a sultry voice.

"No, they can't start without me." He pointed to himself "I'm calling the numbers today."

"I guess we better get moving."

Frenchetta grabbed her keys, locked the door and the two

of them headed to Dulaney Hall. They walked side-by-side, and as she passed some of the other residents, she flashed them a smile.

"I could get used to this," she mumbled.

"What did you say?"

"I just said I gotta get used to all these hallways."

"You'll get used to it. It just takes some time."

Upon arrival, the first person Frenchetta saw was Lily. She was waving and beckoning for Frenchetta to sit with her.

"Looks like you've already made a friend," Norman said.

"We met earlier." She smiled.

"Good for you. She'll keep you company while I'm calling the numbers."

Frenchetta went over to the table where Lily was sitting. She had six cards and several markers.

"Hey, Frenchie, you can sit right by me," she said, moving her bag to the next available seat.

"Thanks." She sat down and hated that she'd agreed to come. This wasn't her idea of spending time with Norman.

"Here you can have two of my cards." Lily sat the cards in front of her.

"Where are the chips?" Frenchetta asked.

"I'm hungry, too. Maybe we can go down to the cafeteria when we're done. I came here straight from the beauty parlor."

"No, not food, I mean the chips for the game."

"Oh, silly goose. We don't use those. We use daubers now. When he calls the number, you just put a little dot on it. When's the last time you played Bingo?"

"I haven't played in years. It's not really my thing."

"Mr. Norman makes it fun. So you'll enjoy it."

"What's his story?"

"He wrote a story. Wow, I had no idea." Lily beamed.

"No, he didn't write a story. Well, at least not to my knowledge."

Frenchetta sighed. "Lily how long has Norman been here? Is he married?" Frenchetta said slowly, hoping that she'd made plain sense to Lily. It was clear that she was a dingy.

"He comes a couple of times a week to help with games and stuff. I don't think he's married, but I can ask him."

"No, that's okay. I was just wondering." Frenchetta grinned with a twinkle in her eye. Hearing that Norman was possibly single was a green light for her to pursue him.

The Bingo game started and Frenchetta loosened up. She had no idea there were so many ways to play. By the time they started the third game, she won in what they called top and bottom, that meant the first and last rows had to be filled in.

"Frenchie, you got it, Bingo, Bingo." Lily stood up and waved her hands getting Norman's attention.

"Alright, Lily, stand up and call off your numbers," said Norman.

"I didn't win. My friend Frenchie won." She patted Frenchetta on the back.

Frenchetta felt her face getting flushed. She was so embarrassed Lily had everyone staring at her. She wasn't used to someone acting in this manner.

"Come on, stand up. Don't be bashful. We're all family," Lily said.

"That's right. We're all family," Norman encouraged.

Frenchetta stood up and rattled off her numbers, and Norman confirmed she was the winner.

"Okay, so what did I win?" Frenchetta asked Lily as she sat down.

"There aren't any prizes. We just play for fun. It's just a great feeling you know you won. You know like on the *Price Is Right* when they call your name to come on down. You run down there with excitement and you never bid the right amount. It's just fun being there."

"How would you know?" Frenchetta inquired.

"I've been on there twice, but never won. My cousin said that's unheard of. But, oh well, it was fun." Lily cackled.

"Yeah, it is. I'm not surprised it happened to you." Frenchetta laughed. She could just see Lily dressed like a hippie running down the aisle screaming and hollering like she'd hit the lottery.

"You wanna go to the cafeteria and get something to eat?"

"No, I think I'm going to head back to my room and get settled. I still need to finish unpacking."

"Okay, well maybe another time. See you later, alligator," she sang.

"See you later, Lily."

"You're supposed to say 'after while crocodile.' That's the song by Billy & His Comets," she informed Frenchetta. "You'll know next time." Lily grabbed her bag and left.

That poor thing. Bless her heart. Frenchetta chuckled to herself as she watched Lily stop at almost every table before she made her way out the door.

"Ain't no telling what she's saying."

"Who?"

Norman startled her.

"Oh, Norman, I was just laughing at Lily. She's something else."

"Yeah, she's a breath of fresh air. Everyone loves her."

"You're kidding. Really?" Frenchetta felt Lily was a little too quirky, and corny.

"Lily has a way with people. She doesn't meet any strangers, and that helps people adjust to their new environment. She's also a big help to me on Thursday nights."

"What happens on Thursday nights?"

"I do a bible study every Thursday night. Lily helps me out by passing out the printouts and she's always willing to open up and share. That helps the others be more comfortable in sharing."

"How sweet of Lily."

"You should join us, that is, if it doesn't interfere with your church night. What church do you attend?"

"I attend Mt. Grove Church and we have bible study on Wednesday nights." She stretched the truth. The truth was she was a member of the church, but she hadn't been since her husband passed away. She knew for a fact their bible study was on Wednesday night, so that was the truth.

"Mt. Grove. That's Pastor Baylor, right?"

"Yes, that's him." Frenchetta smiled.

"He and my uncle are good friends. It's a small world."

"Yeah, it sure is," Frenchetta said nervously.

"Well I hope you enjoyed Bingo. I've got to get out of here. Hopefully, I'll see you on Thursday night."

"I'll be there with bells on." She beamed.

"Sounds like a plan."

Frenchetta watched as Norman walked away.

I gotta get me a new Bible and a notepad, so I can be ready on Thursday night.

"He fine, ain't he?" a younger woman who favored Gabrielle Union said, disturbing her thoughts.

"I beg your pardon." Frenchetta eyed her.

"Look, I saw you checking him out. It's all good. I won't tell a soul. By the way, my name is Tracy," she said popping her gum.

"Frenchetta," she said, not wanting to be bothered.

"Well, good meeting to you, Frenchetta?"

"Are you here visiting your parents?" Frenchetta inquired.

"Um no. I just moved in a few months ago with my husband," she said matter- of- factly.

"Your husband?" Frenchetta was shocked. Tracy looked like she could be in her late forties.

"Aren't we just a little bit nosey?" Tracy laughed.

"No, it's just that you look—"

"I know I look young. I'm proud to be forty-eight, and the only reason they allowed me to move in is because my husband is well over the age limit."

"Oh, I see." Frenchetta scanned the room to see who she could possibly be talking about.

"That's my husband, Earnest, over there in the black Nike warm up." Tracy pointed him out.

She was right. He was well over the age limit. He looked to be over the freeway speed limit too. Earnest had on all Nike gear, and Frenchetta could tell he wasn't comfortable in his outfit, because he kept fidgeting with the jacket and his shoestrings. He even walked like he wasn't used to the shoes.

"Tracy, I've got to get going, but I'm sure we'll see each other again."

"I'm sure we will. Bye."

Frenchetta walked as fast as she could down the hallway to her room. She couldn't wait to call Glo and fill her in on what was going on at Magnolia Gardens.

CHAPTER 7

FRENCHETTA HAD NEVER REALLY SEEN HERSELF AS THE "BUS" type. She much preferred to travel in a car or even on a plane. Somehow, buses always seemed so dirty and cheap. But since half the complex was abuzz about this upcoming Outlet Center and Farmers' Market trip, she decided she might as well make the trip. Otherwise, she'd be alone in the cafeteria for breakfast and lunch.

She arrived at the meeting point at 8:15 a.m., as the event flyer had read. She was surprised to see the doors to the big gray bus slowly closing as she approached the East hallway doors of Magnolia Gardens.

Frenchetta trotted, waving. "Wait!"

She heard the loud puff of air from the bus brakes as the doors parted again. She ascended the stairs and found herself face-to-face with a boy who looked barely old enough to ride a bike. let alone drive a bus.

"Okay, ma'am, you're a little late," he informed her in a

firm tone. "Go ahead and sign in and take a seat." He shoved a clipboard toward her.

"I am not late," Frenchetta insisted. "It said be here at eight-fifteen."

"We *leave* at eight-fifteen," he said. "But it's your first time, so I'll let it slide."

Frenchetta couldn't argue with him. The boy was just doing his job, even if he did take it too seriously. She nodded and followed his directions, nonetheless. If only Keith could take things as seriously at this young man, he might actually get somewhere in life.

She printed and signed her name, as well as listed her cell phone number on the form, accordingly.

"Thank you, Miss..." he read the form, "Davenport?"

"Yes. Frenchetta Davenport."

"All right. My name is Gavin." He stuck out his chest and pointed at his name badge. "Go ahead and find the nearest open seat, please."

Again, Frenchetta obeyed, almost tickled at the boy's pride. She clutched her bag tight to her side so as not to brush those who were seated in the first rows. The first empty seat, however, happened to be next to Buddy.

Buddy patted the empty seat. "You heard the man. Right here!"

She scanned the bus to see if there were any other spots by people she knew. Lily, Zeke, and Norman were already paired up. Tracy, of course, was sitting with Earnest. The only other open seat was at the very back of the bus, which would surely smell of fumes. So, reluctantly, Frenchetta sat next to Buddy, thinking that next time she would be at the meeting point before eight o' clock so she could make sure this never happened again.

"Hello, Miss Frenchie." Buddy smiled, and his wrinkles rolled upward. From the way his skin crinkled, he must have been heavier in his younger years because all his skin was still there. *He should gain weight.*

"Hello, Buddy." The name was so wrong. "What's your real name, may I ask?"

"Only those closest to me get the opportunity to know my government name." He winked at her.

"I just don't feel comfortable calling you Buddy when you're *not* my buddy," Frenchetta said quietly.

"I *could* be." He attempted to put his arm across Frenchetta's shoulder.

She leaned her body all the way into the aisle, swatting his arm away. "I don't think so."

Frenchetta heard snickering from those sitting around her. She felt a tap on her back and turned to see Lily's smiling face.

"Buddy's just a big flirt, Frenchie. He's harmless."

"Well, his flirting is harming me."

Lily laughed. "You are so funny."

Frenchetta rolled her eyes and faced forward again.

"Fren—"

"Look. Buddy." Frenchetta whipped around to face him. "I'm going to save you some time. I don't want to be your woman. I don't want to be your buddy. I don't want to be your *nothin'* except neighbor."

He nodded with a sly grin. "You a hard-to-get one, huh?"

Frenchetta stared at him. Point blank. "I'm a never-gonna-get one, for you."

Unfortunately, Buddy was still grinning.

She shook her head and fished through her purse for her headphones. She hooked them to her phone, pushed the buds into her ears, rested her head on the seat back, and kept her eyes shut until she felt the bus come to a stop about thirty minutes later.

Gavin performed a headcount as they exited the bus and gave a quick speech at the main entrance to the mall. "We'll leave here at eleven o' clock sharp and head on out to the market."

Frenchetta, along with the others, nodded in agreement. There had to be about fifty of them there. *We look like a bunch of old people on a field trip. Wait—we are a bunch of old people on a field trip.*

She laughed to herself at the thought, adjusted her straw hat, and headed off to explore the outlet. Shopping was one thing that Frenchetta enjoyed doing all by herself. Whether looking for clothes, food, shoes, gifts, or whatever, Frenchie didn't want or need a second opinion. It messed up her concentration and took from her enjoyment.

But if Norman were alone, that would be different.

She searched the dispersing crowd for his tall frame and found him amongst a group of men, including Buddy, who were headed for an athletic shoe store.

There was no way she'd risk another moment with Buddy.

Frenchetta spent the hour and a half roaming through the stores, taking in the smells, sounds, and sight of Christmas decorations still in place. Thankfully, the weather was warm enough for her to tolerate a brisk walk between stores.

She quickly assessed, by looking at the prices, that this

outlet mall wasn't much of a discount center. Nonetheless, she found a few bracelets and a cute turquoise and black towel set that would go nicely with her new bathroom.

Before long, browsing through stores and down aisles had her feeling like her old self again. It had been a while since Frenchetta got out like this and shopped just because, not shopping for something that Elroy or the kids needed. She was shopping for herself, just like she'd moved into Magnolia Gardens—for herself.

I'm worth it.

Time at the mall passed quickly. Frenchetta made sure she was back at the meeting spot before pull-away time, so she wouldn't get stuck with Buddy again. This time, she got on first and put her purse down in the seat next to her in the fourth row behind the driver.

When she saw Norman board the bus, she moved her things so he could see the open seat next to her. But he was so busy talking to Lily and another red-headed woman that he didn't see her offer.

Lily again!

She saw Zeke get on the bus, and two people behind him was Buddy. By then, the bus was getting pretty full. Not willing to risk sitting next to Buddy again, Frenchetta said to Zeke, "I've got room here."

"Oh! Don't mind if I do." Zeke sat next to her, and Frenchetta sighed with relief.

He pointed at the bags in her hand. "Looks like you cleaned house."

"Just a few things."

"May I see?"

Frenchetta's brows furrowed. Men didn't usually care to see what women picked up on their shopping sprees.

Zeke said, "I mean, unless it's too private."

"No," Frenchetta agreed, taking out the towels, "it's just towels and stuff." She showed them to Zeke.

"Nice." He nodded. "You have good taste."

"Why thank you. And what did you get?"

"Aaah, nothing. I didn't see anything I liked."

Frenchetta found that hard to believe. The man was dressed in a plaid shirt that had what appeared to be an ink stain on the pocket. And his jeans looked as though he'd been playing in a major league baseball game, sliding into every base. They weren't dirty, but definitely worn and faded—not in a stylish way. Surely there was *something* he could have found at the mall. "Did you go to Nordstrom's Rack?"

"Naw. I don't do too much shopping. Most of my clothes I've had for at least fifteen years."

Frenchetta tried to hide her disapproval, but it must have been written on her face.

Zeke laughed. "You look like I just told you I don't take baths!"

Frenchetta couldn't help but laugh. Thankfully, Zeke joined in.

"Fifteen years, Zeke! That's a long time!"

"Well, when you have a certain style, and you can't find it in the stores anymore—"

"That's because it's *out* of style," Frenchetta informed him, still tickled.

Zeke shook his head. "Plaid is never out of style. And if it did go out of style, it's coming back." He popped the collar of his shirt, which sent Frenchetta into another round of laughter.

She had to stop herself from getting too loud. "Zeke, you are too much."

He shrugged. "I'm just a low-maintenance man. Something my ex-wife didn't appreciate."

Frenchetta raised an eyebrow. "Oh?"

"Yeah. She wanted somebody flashy. Social. Younger."

"Younger?"

"Yeah. She left me for somebody much younger. Said he was more her style."

"Mmmm." Frenchetta rocked her head. "Well, clothes don't make the man."

"Somebody should have told her that."

Frenchetta and Zeke enjoyed a pleasant ride to the Farmers' Market where he showed her which vendor had the best squash and assured her the fresh chicken from Planters Farm was the greatest poultry on earth.

Their conversation was friendly and easy, which was why Frenchetta had no problems sitting next to Zeke on the way back to Magnolia Gardens. Unlike Buddy, Zeke wasn't pushy. He wasn't even flirty. Just nice, like a good friend.

They didn't talk much on the way back. In fact, the bus was markedly quiet. Everyone was tired.

But they were all suddenly filled with a wakening shock when they returned to the center. A collective, fearful gasp conquered the bus. Ambulance lights flashed across everyone's face. Immediately, Frenchetta wondered what had happened and who it had happened to.

"Oh my," Lily cried. "Not another one."

Frenchetta asked Zeke, "Another one?"

"We *are* old here at Magnolia Gardens. Every once in a while, somebody has a bad fall or a reaction to a medicine... or passes away."

Norman prayed out loud, "Lord, have mercy."

CHAPTER 8

THE RESIDENTS HURRIEDLY GATHERED THEIR BAGS TO EXIT the bus. Gavin helped all of the ladies down the three steps and bid them all a farewell. He'd mentioned something about an upcoming outing to a rodeo in the months to come, but that fell on deaf hears.

Lily rushed through the front door and to the front desk to find out what had happened.

She tapped her fingers on the desktop as she waited for Cynthia Nixon, the resident concierge, to finish her phone call.

"Cynthia, who is the ambulance here for?" Lily nervously asked.

"They're here for Irene Maywood, but—"

Lily didn't stay to hear the rest of Cynthia's statement; she ran down the hallway toward her room. Irene and Lily had been neighbors for several years.

Upon arrival to Irene's room, Lily saw the ambulance attendants preparing to roll her out on a gurney. Irene was covered by a white sheet.

"Why y'all got that cover over Irene's face? Is she cold?" Tears rolled down Lily's eyes as she attempted to reach for the cover, but one of the attendants stopped her. Lily heaved uncontrollably.

"Ma'am take a few deep breaths, we don't want you to get yourself worked up," he said.

Norman, Zeke, and Frenchetta rushed by her side to offer comfort. With Buddy in tow.

Norman held Lily in his arms.

"Sir, we're going to take her vital signs just to be safe," a freckle-faced paramedic whose name tag bore the name Slipnoxsky said.

Slipnoxsky and Norman helped her sit down while the other attendants rolled Irene out of the room.

"Noooooooooooooooo!" she screamed and attempted to get up, but couldn't.

"Lily, sweetheart, please try to calm down," Frenchetta said as she rubbed her back.

"Frenchie's right. You don't want to run your pressure up." Zeke patted her shoulder.

"She was my best friend," Lily sobbed.

"The good book says we all gotta go," Buddy chimed in.

"Speaking of going, I think that's what you ought to do, Buddy," Frenchetta spat and cut her eyes at him.

"I'm just saying ..."

"Buddy, now isn't the time," Zeke sternly replied.

"Alright, her pressure's up a tad bit, but that's to be expected under the circumstances. She should check it again in a few hours, just to be safe."

"We have twenty-four hour care here, so we'll make sure she gets it checked again," Norman said.

"I'm sorry for your loss. Take care of yourself." Slipnoxsky shook Lily's hand and left.

"Come on, Lily, let's get you to your room," Zeke said.

"I wanna stay here, so I can be close to Irene," she whined.

"Irene is in your heart, so she's already close to you. Staying here isn't a good idea," Norman stated.

"You can stay with me tonight," Frenchetta offered.

"That's a great idea." Norman nodded his head and thanked Frenchetta.

She smiled at the fact that he'd finally paid her some attention.

"Let's pray for Irene before we leave. Father, in the name of Jesus. Lord, we come to You today asking for peace and comfort in our hearts during this trying time, Thank You for Irene and the times we've had with her. We pray for strength for Lily and all of those who loved and cared about her, and we lift up her family members, as well. In Jesus name. Amen," Norman ended the prayer.

"Amen," they all said in unison.

After getting Lily calmed down, Frenchetta went across the hall to Lily's room to get her something more comfortable to put on.

Lord, all these outfits scream country. She laughed.

She settled on a cow pajama set, with matching underwear garments. Unfortunately, that was the best choice of them all.

"I got you a pair of pajamas. Why don't you freshen up, and I'll make us some tea."

"Frenchie, you're so kind, thank you." Lily hugged her and held on tight as she cried some more.

"It's going to be alright," Frenchetta managed to say, fighting back her own tears.

Lily took the pajamas and went into the bathroom.

Frenchetta sat quietly thinking about what all had taken place. She didn't know what she'd do if she lost her best friend. Glo had been there through all of her good and bad times. She forced the thought out of her mind and busied herself making the tea.

Twenty minutes later, Lily came out of the bathroom. Frenchetta could tell she'd been crying some more; her eyes were red and puffy

"Drink this. It'll make you feel better." Frenchetta handed her a cup of comforting chamomile tea.

The two of them sat on the couch side-by-side.

"Frenchie, thanks for being a friend to me."

"You've shown yourself friendly to me since day one." Frenchetta patted her hand.

Lily had shown herself friendly to her, but truthfully Frenchetta had always kind of tolerated Lily.

"I'd like to get to know you better, my friend." Frenchetta smiled.

"Well there's not a lot to tell. When I was nine years old, I fell in love with cows."

"Hahahahaha, Oh my goodness, Lily."

"What's so funny?" A puzzled Lily asked.

"I wasn't expecting you to go back to your childhood,

that's all." Frenchetta sipped her tea.

"I was taught if you're going to tell a story, start at the beginning," Lily said with a straight face.

Lily went on to tell Frenchetta how she fell in love with cows after visiting her grandparents farm. After her grandfather died, her family moved to the farm to help take care of her grandmother and the land. Her mother inherited the land, but sold it.

"I was devastated." Lily gulped down the rest of her tea.

"I'm sure you were. So where did you move to?"

"We ended up living in the city in some fancy brownstone apartments."

"Why didn't you like the brownstone apartments?" Frenchetta asked as she made her way to the kitchen to fix them some sandwiches.

"The problem wasn't the brownstone, I just don't like the city," Lily pointed out."I couldn't wait to get grown and gone. So after I graduated, I went to college and fell madly in love with Oscar." Her eyes lit up. "We married after two months of dating."

"Two months? That was quick." Frenchetta placed the Hawaiian roll turkey sliders, plates, and condiments on the table.

"When you know it's love, there's no need in waiting." Lily picked up a slider and spread some mustard on it.

"I suppose you're right."

Lily told Frenchetta that she and Oscar bought a house in the country with plenty of land, just like she'd had as a child.

"Do you have any children?" Frenchetta inquired.

"We have three knuckleheads. They, of course, are all grown, living in the city," Lily replied with sadness in her eyes."I haven't seen them in quite some time. They're upset with me for selling my house and land."

"Children are something else; they act like we owe them something." Frenchetta took a bite of her slider.

"Penelope, Lester, and Robert act the same way. I sold the house and the land after Oscar died because none of them came around. Frenchie, those kids plum drained me. I got sick and tired of them expecting me to come running every time they called. Oh, but they won't do the same thing for me," she said in between chews.

"I can definitely relate." Frenchetta refilled their tea.

"Penelope calls more than the boys. I get to talk to my grandson, Brendan, from time to time. He's three." Lily grinned.

"Those phone calls just weren't enough. I got lonesome and tired of waiting around on them to come pay me some attention. Frenchie, that's why I moved here. I'm at peace. Irene was the first person I met when I got here. We moved in on the same day." She choked back her tears.

Frenchetta allowed her to have her moment. She and Lily had more in common than she'd realized. She hadn't heard from Katrina since she'd move in. She, too, wished she could not only receive more calls, but she wanted to see her grandchildren, too.

"This place is certainly peaceful. I love it. I'm glad I decided to move here," Frenchetta admitted.

"I'm glad you did, too. We're all one big happy family. I'll admit I miss my house, but I still go visit from time to time. The new owners have turned it into a bed and breakfast. It's beautiful. It's in Bridges, about an hour away from here. You should come with me the next time I visit," Lily offered.

"I'd love to." Frenchetta smiled.

CHAPTER 9

ON TOP OF THE FACT THAT HIS CAR WASN'T WORKING, Monica had gotten it towed from the parking lot of her apartment complex. In a text-argument, she claimed that was only because her manager told her she had to remove the vehicle from the premises. But Keith knew better. He had parked in the forbidden parking spaces plenty of times—for weeks at a time—without so much as a threat to have his car towed.

It was one thing for Monica to kick him out, but now she was taking vengeance on his car. Not to mention the child support she had threatened.

This girl was taking things too far.

But he couldn't think about her at the moment. He had to get some cash. Fast. The only person who might be in a position to give him hundreds of dollars was his sister, Katrina. She and her husband both had college degrees and good jobs. They had that good old American house and two kids and two cars. Hopefully, they hadn't spent all their tax check yet.

Since she lived in a larger city, Keith was able to Uber to the nearest bus hub and then hop a bus to her side of town. He walked about a quarter of a mile to her house, backpack and all. Since it was six in the evening by the time he made it, he figured Katrina should have been home.

But he was wrong. When he rang the doorbell of her two-story cookie-cutter house, there was no answer, only the bark of a small dog he didn't even know his sister had. The blonde Yorkie yapped and bounced in the tiny window just to his right.

For a moment, he envied that dog. It had a nice, warm place to stay. A family. "You don't know how lucky you are," he whispered as the dog continued barking.

Keith pretended to punch the window, taunting the dog through the glass.

The Yorkie began to growl and scratch.

It was just like his sister to get some kind of froo-froo dog. She wasn't too much different from their mom sometimes. Katrina could act funny. He had to be careful about how he posed the request and be cautious about how much information to share. He also needed to ask her without her husband present. But at the same time, Katrina might say something crazy. Like, "I need to talk to my husband first," since he'd be asking for a large sum.

It was a good thing he'd had some time to wait before his sister came home from work. He needed all that time to concoct a convincing plea. Keith sat down on the porch step and thought.

About a half-hour later, he heard the garage door squeaking and saw his sister's red BMW SUV coming around the corner.

Man, I wish I had one of those.

His father always told Keith that he could have whatever he wanted in life if he was willing to work for it. And then his father would point out how Katrina was setting a great example for him, making a great name for the Davenports in school. "She's blazing a path for you, son."

The thing is, he didn't want to go down that same path. Katrina was one of those people who loved reading, loved school, loved learning. She was a natural-born student. College must have been a breeze for her, and now that she had a job researching at some big biochemical company, she probably enjoyed that nerdy job all day.

Yeah, Katrina had it easy because she naturally wanted to do things the normal way.

But not Keith. He didn't want a boring, normal life. He wanted it all!

The garage door was all the way up now. Katrina stopped before pulling in. "Hey, Keith. What are you doing here?" Her precise eyebrows drew in tightly, making her baby-face appear more stern than he could remember her looking in a long time. She must have been stressed out from that desk job she had, though Keith could never understand why people who sat all day would actually be tired after work.

He shrugged. "I'm... in a bad way."

She looked him up and down. "Whatchu mean 'in a bad way'?"

"Down on my luck."

She blinked. His sister seemed to be studying him, as though he were some homeless bum who'd shown up on her step. Finally, she sighed. "Come on in."

Keith followed her into the garage, then into the house. She put her computer bag and purse down on the kitchen hutch. Keith did the same.

"You can fix yourself something to eat. There's lunch meat and bread." She pointed at the refrigerator and the bread box. "Chips in the pantry. Let me change clothes real quick and we can talk. But we can't talk long. I have to go pick up Madison from soccer practice in about half an hour, then it's homework, dinner, and baths from there."

"Where's Jonathan?" Keith asked.

"He'll be home some time later on this evening after Kevan's karate class."

Great. He'd have some time to talk to his sister alone. He made himself at home and built a double-decker sandwich with a plate full of Doritos. He also grabbed a soda from the smaller part of the high-tech refrigerator.

Katrina returned wearing a sweatshirt and stretchy pants, instead of the navy blue suit she'd worn to work. "So what's up?" She sat down at the kitchen table and took one of his chips.

"Well..." He took a bite of his sandwich.

A flash of light shone from her watch.

Katrina raised her wrist to read the screen. "Oh great. Madison left her cleats at home. I have to leave now. How much money do you need, Keith?"

"Dang," he said, leaning back in his chair. "How you know this is about money?"

"Because that's the only time anyone hears from you. Now, how much?"

Keith shook his head. "A lot. My engine blew up. And my car is in the pound. I need five hundred just to get it out, and a couple of thousand to get it fixed."

"Twenty five hundred dollars!" Katrina shrieked. "Do I look like Wells Fargo to you?"

"Naw, but I'm sayin'... you ain't poor." He looked around the spacious kitchen and dining area.

"I ain't rich, either. I have bills. We just got back from a cruise, so Jonathan and I don't have a whole bunch of zeros in our accounts, my brother."

"But you got a way to get zeros, which is more than what I have." Keith pointed.

"That's because we work two fifty-hour jobs every week, hello."

"Here you go," Keith fussed, eating the sandwich. "Sound just like Momma."

Katrina reached for another chip, but Keith pulled the plate away.

"How you stop me from taking one of *my* chips from *my* plate in *my* house?" Katrina laughed.

But Keith didn't see anything funny. Somehow, everybody thought he was a joke, like he didn't matter. "I need *all* these chips. No telling when I might have another meal."

"Okay, well take the whole bag. But I don't have twenty-five hundred dollars to give you. And I have to go pick up Madison now. You already asked Momma?"

"Yeah. She said no. She's using up all her money at that fancy old folks home she moved to."

"Is she enjoying it?"

Keith scoffed, "She's enjoying it too much. Spending up all our inheritance. Don't you care that we're gonna be broke because of her?"

"Keith, you're broke *now*."

"Really? You gonna kick me while I'm down?"

"All I'm saying is, if Momma seems happier than she's been in a long time, I say leave her alone."

"What am I supposed to do in the meantime?"

"Get a job, maybe?" Katrina suggested sarcastically.

She quickly grabbed some chips from Keith's plate before he could pull them away. "I can give you a hundred." She pulled two fifty-dollar bills from her pocket and slapped them on the table.

"A hundred?" Keith whined.

"Yes, a hundred. Take it or leave it. And make up your mind because I gotta go."

What good would a hundred dollars do in this situation? And if she had a hundred dollars in cash lying around the house, she probably had at least a hundred more, not to mention what she could probably get from an ATM.

"So, that's all you got? A hundred dollars?" he quizzed.

"That's all I have to give."

She was probably lying. Nonetheless, he took the money. Shoved it in his pocket.

"Uh, you're welcome."

"Whatever." Keith grabbed his bags.

These people, his family, were driving him to the other side. Now, he'd have to do what he had to do to survive.

CHAPTER 10

"Ms. Frenchie, I saw you over there working it. You still got a few moves." Tracy laughed.

"A few, honey, speak for yourself." Frenchetta snapped her fingers.

"Alright now, I'm scared of you."

"And you should be." She chuckled. Frenchetta and Tracy had just left a line dance class. The two had become friends a few months back and hanging out with Tracy was always fun.

"Let's go get a smoothie," Tracy suggested as they walked down the hallway.

"I need to go wash my hair for tonight."

"What's going on tonight?"

"Norman is leading bible study tonight at six. I planned to be there." Frenchetta grinned.

"Ummmm hmm you'll be studying something, but it won't be the Bible." Tracy gulped loudly."

"Will you hush before someone hears you," Frenchetta fussed.

"Okay, okay, okay. I'm sorry, but I'm so excited for you. You about to be like Stella and get your groove back."

"Let's hope so," Frenchetta said with a beam in her eyes.

"Instead of washing your hair, maybe you should change your look. Do something different. Like cut your hair."

"I'm not cutting my hair. I like my hair," she said, annoyed by Tracy's suggestion.

"Short hair makes you look younger, and I think if you get a short cut like Halle Berry, it'll be cute on you. It's just hair. It will grow back," she pointed out.

Frenchetta pondered on the idea; she'd had long hair all her life and had only allowed her beautician to trim her ends.

"A new haircut will give you a new attitude," Tracy added.

"Okay, I'll do it. But you have to come with me."

"Great, Melba can probably hook you up right now. Let's go see."

Tracy and Frenchetta went to the elevator and to the second floor where the beauty shop was.

This was Frenchetta's first time coming to the shop. It was very small; there were only eight stations with shampoo bowls, and hair dryers lining the wall.

Tracy spotted Melba, and she and Frenchetta made their way to the back where she was working.

She finished rolling a lady's hair and placed her under the dryer.

Frenchetta admired Melba's hair—cut short with small curls and burgundy highlights.

"Melba, this is my friend Ms. Frenchie. She wants to get a haircut and style. Can you fit her in?"

"Nice to meet you, Ms.Frenchie. I can start right now while Ms. Harris is under the dryer," Melba said. "Do you know what you want?"

"It's nice meeting you, too, I actually like your hair. But I don't want my hair shaved in the back."

"That's not a problem. I won't cut yours as short as mine."

Frenchetta sat in the chair, and Melba placed a cape around her. Tracy sat in the seat across from her and grabbed a magazine.

"Aren't you going to wash my hair first?" Frenchetta inquired.

"Dry-cutting is what's best for your hair, and it gives you more volume. I promise, I'm going to take care of yo. No worries," she assured Frenchetta.

Holding true to her promise, Melba had given Frenchetta a fabulous new look. Her short jazzy cut made her look younger.

"I love it, Melba, I absolutely love it," Frenchetta said, staring into the mirror.

"I'm glad you like it." Melba smiled.

"I told you Melba got them skills," Tracy stated.

Frenchetta charged her cut to her room, and she and Tracy headed back downstairs. She only had an hour to figure out what she was going to wear to bible study.

"We have to make sure you have the right outfit, 'cause all eyes will definitely be on you," Tracy said.

"I was thinking about wearing my little black dress."

"Black dress? Honey, you ain't in mourning. You need some color."

"Oh boy, here comes trouble," Tracy warned her. Buddy was walking up the hallway towards them.

"Baby, your name must be cholesterol, 'cause you got my blood pressure rising." Buddy did a double take checking out Frenchetta's new look.

Tracy laughed, but Frenchetta didn't acknowledge him.

"That's alright, I'll get with you later. You'll give in soon," he called after her.

"Oh my, somebody's nose is wide open," Tracy yelped.

"Well, open or closed, that ain't what I'm fishing for. Old trout." Frenchetta chuckled.

Frenchetta and Tracy decided she should wear her green low cut, fit and flare swing dress, with gold accessories and her gold pumps.

Doing a once-over in the mirror, she grabbed her new Bible, pen set and notepad, and went to bible study. She was about five minutes late, but she'd planned it that way so she could make a grand entrance.

"Frenchie, you're just in time. We're about to start our lesson. Glad you decided to join us," Norman said.

Several of the other residents were whispering, and she knew she was the subject. When she looked in their direction, they all became quiet. Frenchetta sat at the table with Lily and Zeke.

"You look nice. A little over-dressed, but nice," Zeke whispered.

"Thanks." She smiled.

"Tonight we're going to talk about putting God first in your life Turn your Bibles to Matthew 6:33," Norman instructed. "Who would like to read it?"

"I'll read it," said one of the residents in the back. "But seek ye first the kingdom of God and his righteousness; and all these things shall be added unto you."

"So what is this scripture trying to tell us?" Norman asked.

Lily raised her hand and waited for Norman to acknowledge her

"Go ahead, Lily. Feel free to answer."

"I think God is telling us to get our priorities together," Lily said.

"Not only that, but to put Him first," Zeke added.

"Both of you are correct. God wants us to put Him before everything. We spend time focusing on what we have. Cars, money, clothes, friends, and others things and forget all about God. You can focus on all of that stuff and still be empty and lost because those things are only temporary."

Frenchetta thought about what Norman said. She'd focused on all of those things and was still feeling empty. Something was indeed missing from her life.

"Seek a personal relationship with God that will bring you into right standing with Him. He wants to be first and if you put Him first, you won't have to worry as much as you do," Norman said. "Ask yourself this question: is God sitting on the throne of my life or is He on the outside, only able to get in when I allow Him to?"

Frenchetta paid close attention. She felt ashamed, because the only time she talked to God was when she needed Him.

"God's promise to us is that if we seek Him with our whole heart, He will supply all of our needs according to His riches in glory. Do you have enough faith to believe that?" Norman asked.

Frenchetta heard several residents say yes. She simply nodded her head.

"If you're unsure, then ask Him to give you the faith to put Him first and faith to trust that He'll supply your needs."

Norman talked a little bit more about God supplying needs and gave a few more scripture references. Lily and Zeke were taking notes and Frenchetta wrote all the verses down on her note pad, too.

"Before we end, I'd like for us to stand and hold hands for the prayer," Norman stated.

"Father God, thank You for tonight's lesson. Lord, we seek You with our whole hearts. I ask that You continue to bless all of us how You see fit, and I pray that our faith is strengthened so that we'll trust Your plans for our lives and trust that You will supply all of our needs. Lord, You are our hope and our confidence, there's none like You and none greater and we give You all of the glory and honor in Jesus name, Amen."

"Amen," Everyone chimed in.

"I hope you enjoyed bible study?" Norman said to Frenchetta as she gathered her things.

"Yes, I really did," she admitted.

"Well I hope I said something to help you with your walk with Him." He smiled.

"You did, and thanks," she said as she left.

Frenchetta didn't know what had come over her. She didn't wait to talk to Lily or Zeke. She walked back to her room alone. After taking off her clothes and makeup, she turned on her lamp and sat onside of her bed and looked at her note pad. Norman had given them Proverbs 3:5-6 as one of the scripture references. She flipped through her message Bible and found the scripture.

Trust God from the bottom of your heart; don't try to figure out everything on your own.

Listen for God's voice in everything you do, everywhere you go; he's the one who will keep you on track.

Lord, I know that I haven't been trusting You. I been running around doing my own thing. Please forgive me. Please show me how to trust You more. Lord, and if it's not asking too much, please let Katrina reach out to me and please watch over Keith. Amen.

CHAPTER 11

FRENCHETTA HAD FOUND THE PERFECT TIME TO DO HER laundry—at 5:30 on Tuesday afternoons. Everyone at Magnolia Gardens was busy playing double-Bingo, trying to win little trinkets and prizes. If not, they were just finishing up dinner. Frenchetta had learned that if she got to the cafeteria a little before 4:45, she could be at the front of the line and be finished in time to have the laundry room all to herself.

She liked Magnolia Gardens well enough so far, but she had to admit to herself that it was nice to not be surrounded by so many people she hardly knew, all the time. She could always go to her room to get away, but it wasn't nearly as expansive as her house. A person could go crazy in that small space.

Frenchetta laughed at herself as she loaded the washer with white clothes. She realized her arguments made no sense. She wanted to be alone in the washroom, but not too alone in her room.

She supposed she was still "adjusting." That's what they had called it when she'd gone through new-resident's orientation. They had said to give your mind and your body a few months to get used to the surroundings and the pace of things.

Frenchetta had only been there for a matter of months. She'd give herself some more time.

After starting her clothes in two washers, Frenchetta sat down in the rocking chair and grabbed an AARP Magazine. She rocked herself through reading a few informative articles. One was about life insurance and making sure she had appropriate beneficiaries. The second article listed the top ten cruises for seniors. They even had cruises for single seniors looking for mates with which to spend the second half of their lives.

"What in the world?" Frenchetta gasped. She couldn't imagine putting herself out there like that. "Those people must be desperate." The last thing Frenchetta wanted in her life was another husband. Elroy had been good. Close to perfect. Yes, he had worked a lot, but he was a good provider. He'd never mistreated her, never called her out of her name. And on top of all that, he had loved her. That was way more than what she could say for a lot of men, from what she could see with her friends and their marriages.

Nonetheless, Frenchetta went ahead and read the full article about the cruises, which included testimonials from people who had actually participated in each cruise. When she got to the commentary about the seniors' match-making cruise, she was surprised to find an attractive couple touting the benefits of not only the cruise, but of remarrying.

The man was a widower. His wife had died suddenly of an aneurism. The woman didn't go into what happened with her first husband, but it sounded like they were both getting married for a second time. Frenchetta read: *I had given up on love at my age. When my daughter bought me the tickets for the cruise, she didn't tell me it was for seniors looking to be paired up. I probably wouldn't have come. But I'm so glad I didn't know up until I boarded the ship. I decided to just have a great time and enjoy myself... until I met Jeff.*

"Hmph. I'll say," Frenchetta scoffed. She had been wrong about the people being desperate, but she wasn't so sure about the idea of falling in love at their age. How many times can you find true love in life?

By the time she finished reading through all the articles that interested her, it was time for her clothes to go into the dryer.

"Frenchetta Davenport, please come to the front desk. You have a visitor."

Frenchetta stood straight up. *A visitor?* She was sure she'd heard her name, clear as day, over the loud speaker.

She quickly stuffed the clothes into the dryers and headed to the reception desk, where her eyes nearly began to water. *Katrina! The kids!*

"Hey!" Frenchetta nearly yelled like a country person sitting on the porch. "What are you all doing here?"

"Grandma Frenchie!" Madison shrieked. She and her younger brother, Kevan, rushed into Frenchie's waiting arms.

"Oh! What are you all doing here?" The children felt so good in her embrace. They smelled of outdoors—as all kids probably did at that time on a warm day—but she didn't care. They were her grandkids. And they were there to see her.

Katrina ambled over after them, wearing a big smile. "Momma, look at you! Your hair!"

With the kids still clinging to her side, Frenchetta asked, "You like it?"

"I *love* it! Makes you look younger. Spunky. Feisty."

"You think?" Frenchetta asked shyly.

"Most definitely. Daddy would have loved it, too."

"Aww, thank you, baby."

Katrina joined the hug.

"I'm so glad to see you," Frenchetta said, hoping the emotion wouldn't seep through her voice. She didn't want to be one of those overly sentimental people.

"Good to see you, too, Momma."

Katrina was looking good. Her skin was smooth and supple; she'd been drinking her water as Frenchetta had taught her while growing up. Though Katrina's eyes said she was tired, it was to be expected. Two kids, a full-time job outside of the home, and being a wife had to be exhausting. Frenchetta had also tried to instill a love for homemaking in her daughter. But Katrina was one of those career-having types, so maybe she wouldn't have to be so tired trying to be Superwoman.

"What brings you all here?"

"Well, I was thinking about you. Actually, I was talking about you," Katrina said. "We need to talk."

"Grandma, can we see your room?" Kevan asked.

"You sure can. Here's my key," Frenchetta said, taking the plastic spiral bracelet off her wrist. "Room 1081."

Madison grabbed the key.

"Don't run," Katrina ordered.

Frenchetta was happy to see the children obey.

She and Katrina took a seat on the couch in the lobby. "What's on your mind, Katrina?"

Katrina opened her mouth to say something, but then she stopped. Peered into Frenchetta's face.

"What's wrong?" Frenchetta asked.

Katrina's eyes got misty as she said, "You're... happy. Aren't you?"

Frenchetta smiled. "Yes. I guess as happy as I can be."

"Are you making friends?"

"Yes, I've met a few people. We could become friends."

"You getting out?"

"They have a lot of outings for us here. Some of them are fun."

Katrina sat back. "You know, Momma, I came here to try to talk you into maybe leaving this place. Keith is panicking. He had me thinking you had lost your mind and were wasting all your money. But now that I'm here, seeing you has changed my mind. If you like this place, I love it."

"Thank you, baby. I'm glad *somebody* understands."

Frenchetta hugged her daughter again.

The children came fast-walking back to them. "Grandma! You have the best house! I could totally live here forever! This place is beautiful!" Madison gushed. She twirled around in circles. Kevan followed suit. They twirled and twirled until they started to stumble from dizziness.

"Who are these beautiful children?"

Frenchetta recognized Lily's voice. Instead of overlooking

Lily, she invited her to the couch. "Lily, come meet my daughter and my grandchildren."

"Oh!" Lily's eyes shined. "How wonderful!"

"They just dropped by. Out of nowhere."

Lily took it upon herself to hug the children as though she hadn't been in the pleasant company of kids in a long time.

Soon, the cafeteria began to empty, which brought a small crowd over to Frenchetta, Katrina, and the children. Apparently, the residents of Magnolia Gardens were ecstatic about youngsters. They all stood around taking turns asking the children questions: *How old are you? What grade are you in? What do you want to be when you grow up? Which one of you is the boss?* Then, they all waited for the answers with baited breath. The kids ate up the attention.

Everyone complimented Frenchetta on her well-behaved, brilliant grandchildren and her beautiful daughter. Frenchetta took it all in with pride and gratefulness.

Far too soon, Katrina said, "We've gotta get on out of here. Homework awaits."

"Awww," the children balked. "Can we stay?"

Frenchetta seized the opportunity. "You're welcome to come back real soon."

"I'll teach you how to play a guitar," Buddy offered Kevan.

"And I make a mean batch of chocolate chip cookies," Lily offered.

Somehow, the residents seemed to sense Frenchetta's desperate attempt to ensure that her family would return.

"We'll be back soon, Momma. I promise."

One thing Frenchetta knew about kids—once a parent made a promise, children didn't rest until it was fulfilled.

"I look forward to it."

Frenchetta glided back to the laundry room on cloud nine. *My family came to see me!*

Suddenly, she remembered the prayer. She had asked God for this, and He had answered. Not only did she see Katrina, she'd also seen her grandchildren. The Lord had actually listened and answered beyond her imagination.

Wow, God. You really do care about me.

She could hardly fold clothes for the tears in her eyes.

CHAPTER 12

FRENCHETTA HAD BEEN LOOKING FORWARD TO TAKING A trip this afternoon outside of the group. Although she loved her new-found family, she still missed hanging out. As of late she'd only left to go to the local store to pick up personal items or to the grocery store if she felt like doing some cooking. Most of her time was spent with Lily, Tracy, and Zeke.

Three nights ago she'd cooked a big pot of her homemade chili and invited Lily and Zeke over to share some with her.

"This chili so hot, my nose running," Lily said. But that didn't stop her from eating it.

"Frenchie, this is really good; the best chili I've ever had," Zeke complimented.

She packed both of them to-go containers and promised to fix some more soon.

Today she and Lily were driving to Bridges to check out

Lily's old home. Frenchetta was always accused of overdressing, so she decided to wear a burgundy warm-up suit and her Sketchers.

Frenchetta was looking forward to the trip because Glo was tagging along. Glo had planned to visit her and instead of canceling her visit, Lily insisted that Frenchetta invite her, too.

The phone on her desk rang, and she knew it was from the front desk because she hadn't given that number to anyone. All of her family and friends had her cell number.

"Hello," she answered.

"Ms. Davenport, you have a guest. Mrs. Gloria Young," the attendant said.

"Yes, I'll be right there." Frenchetta hung up the phone, grabbed her purse and walked down to the lobby to meet up with Glo.

"Girl, I'm loving the new look," Glo said and hugged Frenchetta.

"I figured I'd switch it up for a while."

"Well, honey it's a cute switch. I'm scared of you." She laughed.

"Come on, let me show you my new place," Frenchetta said and they both left the lobby, heading back to Frenchetta's room.

"Ahem, ahem." Buddy cleared his throat, trying to get Frenchetta's attention as she and Glo passed by his room. He was standing in his doorway with a pair of jeans and a t-shirt that said *Bustin' Loose* on it.

"Frenchie, you ain't gon introduce me to your friend?"

"Buddy, please go away." Frenchetta rolled her eyes and she and Glo went inside her room.

"Who in the world was that?" Glo asked.

"Nobody, just a trifling old man that gets on my last nerve." Frenchetta sighed.

"That shirt should say Bustin Loose at the seams," Glo hollered.

"Ain't that the truth? Shirt fitting him like he in a wet t-shirt contest," Frenchetta laughed.

"You got this place looking great. How are you settling in?"

"I really like it here. I've met some great people, and the other day Katrina and the kids came to see me. Glo, I was so excited. I feel like God placed me here to put my family back in place," she stated.

"Frenchie, that's great. I'm so happy for you. Have you heard anything from Keith?"

"No, I haven't, but I guess no news is good news. It's in God's hands."

"Those are the best hands to me. I'm glad things are turning around for you."

"Slowly, but surely."

The sudden sound of knuckles rapping on the door startled Frenchetta.

"Frenchetta, it's me, Lily. Open up." She knocked again.

"Lily, why in the world are you knocking like someone's after you?" Frenchetta asked.

"I'm just excited. Let's shake, rattle and roll. You must be Glo. Come on, Glo, let's go." Lily giggled.

"Good meeting you, Lily," Glo said, checking out Lily's leopard print tights, cowboy boots, and green caterpillar sweatshirt. Glo glanced at Frenchetta and all she could do was laugh. Glo was a fashionista and prided herself on her attire. Today she wore a pair of jeans with a velvet wine-colored top and a pair of velvet loafers to match.

Frenchetta and Gloria followed Lily through the garage. Frenchetta hadn't thought what type of vehicle Lily might own.

"Lord, please don't let it be a huge contraption of a car," Frenchetta whispered a silent prayer.

Her nerves settled when they arrived at a navy blue PT Cruiser.

"What station are we listening to?" Glo asked as she and Lily sang, "I *said your love keeps lifting me.*"

"It's the Smokie Robinson station," Lily answered.

"Higher and higher," they all sang.

Frenchetta was glad that Lily and Glo were getting along well.

"Jackie Wilson is one of my favorite singers of all times," Lily said when the song ended.

"I love him and the Temptations," Glo stated.

"That's when music meant something," Frenchetta chimed in.

They sang and drove through the piney woods of Bridges. Frenchetta had heard of Bridges, but had never been there before. Seeing the cows, horses, fields of beautiful land was breathtaking.

Lily turned into the driveway where the arrow pointed towards J & M Bed & Breakfast.

"What does the J & M stand for?" Frenchetta asked.

"It's the owners' initials, James & Marita," Lily said.

The bed and breakfast was a light grey, two story Victorian-styled home with a wrap-around porch.

"Oh I love those rocking chairs," Glo said as Lily pulled up in the yard and parked her PT Cruiser.

"Lily, this is beautiful." Frenchetta was in awe of the grounds and seeing the winter jasmine.

"Wait til you see inside."

Glo and Frenchetta followed Lily up the three steps to the front door.

"Lily, it's so good to see you," a white-haired, medium-built woman, with rubber boots on, greeted her.

"It's good to see you, too. I brought a couple friends with me to check the place out. This is Frenchie and Glo." She smiled.

"Well, come on in, Frenchie and Glo. It's good to meet you. I'm Marita."

"Good to meet you, too," they both said and followed Marita inside to the dining room area.

"Would you ladies like some lemonade?" Marita offered.

"How about a glass of teamolade," Lily suggested.

"Teamolade, you mean half tea and half lemonade." Frenchetta laughed.

"I was wondering what she meant." Glo chuckled.

"Alrighty then. Three glasses of teamolade coming right up," Marita said.

The ladies drank their beverages and Marita took them on a tour of the B & B. The four bedrooms were decorated beautifully. All of the rooms had high poster beds, but Frenchetta's favorite was the room with the white Victorian antique poster canopy bed. The bedding was all white with lace, and the room had a lavender fragrance.

"I'm claiming this as my room," Frenchetta said.

"Anytime you want to get away, it's yours," Marita offered.

"Let's head out back. I want y'all to see my woosah spot. I know it's cold, so we won't be out there long," Lily said.

"Your *woosah* spot?" Glo eyed Lily.

"Yeah, it's where I clear my head and take a breather. I do it when I'm frustrated, too," Lily said as they made their way down the stairs.

"Oh, okay, that makes sense," Glo replied.

"You should try it the next time something is bothering you. You stop, take a few moments to release, and say woosah," Lily demonstrated.

"Lily, girl, you are something else," Frenchetta said.

Lily took them to the backyard area where there was an open fireplace with soft leather chairs and also a fire pit for those who may have wanted to make s'mores.

"I usually make a small fire and sit out here for hours. Just me and God, " Lily said.

"We definitely need to come back when it's not too cold," Frenchetta replied, zipping up her jacket. She 'd left her wrap in the car.

"I agree," Glo chimed in.

When they went back inside, Marita had prepared a light lunch for them that consisted of tuna salad, fruit, crackers, and cheese.

"Marita, you must tell me what's in this tuna salad," Glo said between chews.

"It's really good," Frenchetta commented.

"I use sour cream, ranch, and Dijon mustard along with the mayo, it gives it a different taste." Marita smiled.

"I thought I tasted some sour cream," Lily stated as she got a few more crackers.

They sat and ate for about an hour or so, and Marita packed them all a goodie bag to take back with them.

On their way home, Lily stopped by Meg's Country Store for them to do a little shopping.

They all bought scented candles, throw blankets, old fashioned candies, and Lily bought a pair of socks with frogs on them.

"I thought you said you were going to save those for later?" Frenchetta asked Glo, who had almost devoured her fried apple pie.

"Girl, they are too good, and besides Jake eats up everything from me. I can't have nothing to myself," she said.

"Lily, I truly enjoyed this outing. Thanks for inviting me," Frenchetta said as they headed back to Magnolia Gardens.

"And thank you for inviting me, too," Glo stated.

"Thank the both of you for coming. I enjoyed the company. I look forward to doing this again, and the next time we'll spend the night."

"Sounds like a plan," Frenchetta replied.

"I'm in," Glo agreed.

"Cool, we'll be the Golden Girls part 2!" Lily beamed.

Frenchetta and Glo whooped. Frenchetta was glad that both of her friends were getting along and that the trip went well.

The drive home came faster than they all wanted it to.

Frenchetta and Lily both hated to see Glo go. As they all walked through the lobby for Glo to leave, they saw Buddy.

"Frenchetta, I missed you. Come spend some time with big daddy." He grinned.

"Woosah," Frenchetta, Lily, and Glo all said in unison and laughed.

CHAPTER 13

FOR THE FIRST TIME SINCE SHE'D MOVED INTO MAGNOLIA Gardens, Frenchetta woke up fully aware of where she was, without a moment's confusion. This was her new home. Room 1081. Three hot meals prepared for her every day. Numerous activities throughout the week, trips here and there with her peers. And even a new friend now. Goofy, positive Lily, of all people.

Frenchetta reached over onto her nightstand and checked the monthly calendar. The square for the day only had two lines worth of activity. That was rare for Magnolia Gardens. But every now and then there was a slow day. Frenchetta looked forward to relaxing. She would only be taking in a movie in the theater. The center was playing one of her all-time favorite movies, *The Notebook*, as part of the Valentine's month movie marathon.

She shuffled out of bed and headed toward her bathroom to get ready for the day.

For breakfast, in the cafeteria, she chose a cinnamon crunch bagel with honey almond spread. A fruit medley rounded out the plate. She had to be careful at Magnolia Gardens or all that good food would end up on her hips.

Following breakfast, Frenchetta spent about an hour in the library, where she picked a book and began reading. She'd always like long, emotion-packed novels. Now, she had the time to enjoy herself. Her life. Even better, Katrina and the kids had come by for another visit a few days earlier. They had stayed a whole hour.

Life was good again. *Now, if only Keith would get himself together, life would be close to perfect.*

The movie was scheduled to start at ten-thirty, so Frenchetta arrived a few minutes ahead of time. The smell of freshly popped popcorn filled the theater already. She scooped herself a bag of it, pumped a spray of butter, and sprinkled nacho cheese seasoning on top of her snack.

After greeting a few of her fellow residents, she took a seat on the fifth row back and settled in for a good story. The lights dimmed and the show began with a few announcements from Magnolia Gardens management, thanking them for their stay and letting them know of upcoming events.

"This seat taken?"

Frenchetta looked up and smiled at Zeke's friendly face. Though it was dark in the room, she could still see his friendly grin.

"Go right ahead."

She really didn't care who sat next to her, so long as it wasn't Buddy.

Zeke sat to her right just as the opening scene began to play.

"Have you seen this before?" he whispered into her ear.

The closeness of his breath, the quick pull of air, took Frenchetta by surprise. She hadn't been that close to a man in years. Still, she managed to answer, "Many times."

"I haven't."

"Well, you're in for a treat," Frenchetta said, taking in more of her popcorn.

Frenchetta hoped Zeke wasn't one of those people who talked through the whole movie, asking questions and making commentary on every scene. She figured might as well tell him ahead of time because she was not going to let him ruin this movie for her. "Zeke, I don't talk during movies. *Good* movies."

"Me, either," he agreed. "So this better be good."

Frenchetta rolled her neck. "It's one of the best! I wouldn't be sitting here if it wasn't."

Zeke put an index finger over his lips, signaling her to be quiet. "Watch the show."

No he didn't! Frenchetta rolled her eyes at him and faced forward again, laughing on the inside at Zeke's playfulness.

When the sad parts of the movie played, Frenchetta couldn't hold back her tears. She stole a glance at Zeke and saw his shining eyes, too. Though he wasn't crying, his eyes were definitely watering.

The final scene brought a sniffle from him.

Frenchetta was nearly in ugly cry mode by then. This was her first time watching the movie since Elroy died, and it probably wasn't a good idea. True love was so rare. She'd had it once, like those characters in the movie, and it was over for her now. Being held, kissed, caressed. Being wanted, remembered, thought of fondly. All that was a part of her past now. And it didn't help that she was living in a senior living center. Just a few steps away from a nursing home. Would she grow old alone? Would there be anyone to share her last days with? Who would tell hers and Elroy's story?

When the credits began to roll, the lights came back on. Residents began to file out, but Frenchetta stayed in place, unable to move at the moment.

"You were right. That was pretty good," Zeke said.

"Too good," Frenchetta agreed. "That's the first time I've seen this movie since my husband died. He served in the military, too. We had a great love story."

"Yeah?" Zeke asked.

"Yeah. He was a good man. And I miss him every day. It's hard, you know?"

"Can't say that I do," Zeke admitted. "I haven't buried a spouse, but I did bury a child. So I can imagine."

Frenchetta gasped and put a hand on Zeke's arm. "Oh, I'm so sorry to hear about your...was it a son or a daughter?"

"My daughter."

Frenchetta could see the pain ripping through the lines on Zeke's face.

"She was six years old. Ruptured appendix. Happened so fast, we didn't know what hit us."

Suddenly, Frenchetta felt ashamed. There she was grieving over the death of someone who had lived a full, happy life, when there were others who had lost loved ones far too soon.

Zeke continued, "I don't think my wife ever recovered from our daughter's death."

"I don't think you ever recover from something like that," Frenchetta said. "You just find a new normal."

"Yeah." Zeke nodded. "I think you're right. And you hold tight to the Lord. That's the only way I made it through."

Frenchetta nodded. She hadn't exactly clung to God when Elroy died. But if that's what it would take, she was willing to try because watching these sad love stories was taking her to a place she didn't want to go again. For real.

He stood and stretched. "You ready for lunch?"

"I suppose so."

He held out his hand to help Frenchetta up.

Though she actually didn't need any assistance, Frenchetta allowed him to help her anyway.

It made sense for them to stay in each other's presence during lunch, where they talked more about the movie and their own lives. Frenchetta learned that Zeke and his wife had once been very much in love, but their daughter's death was the beginning of how things unraveled.

Frenchetta surprised herself by sharing some of the ups and downs of her own marriage, like her husband's bout with stomach cancer, which nearly drove them to divorce. He had gotten so mean and distant during his illness, excluding her from his fight and even lashing out at her in anger.

When they went to counseling later, Frenchetta learned that this was Elroy's way of coping with the disease. He didn't want his wife to witness his weakness. Also, rather than pull her into his pain, he had attempted to push her away, so that losing him might be easier.

"It was weird, but that was how he viewed it," she said.

"I'm a man. I understand his point."

"Well, anyway, the counseling helped us. Did you and your wife go to counseling?"

"No," Zeke said with a shake of his head. "She wanted to, but I didn't see the use. If I had it to do over again, I would have. But back then, I was too hard-headed, thought I knew everything. Hindsight is twenty-twenty."

"You can say that again," Frenchetta agreed.

Once they finished with lunch, they walked out the doorways side-by-side.

"Thanks for letting me join you today," Zeke said.

"My pleasure. It was nice talking to you."

"You're easy to talk to," Zeke noted. "I like that in a friend."

Frenchetta smiled. "Me, too."

"See you later, ma'am." He dismissed himself with a gentleman's nod.

"Yeah. See you later, Zeke" Frenchetta whispered under her breath.

CHAPTER 14

When Maxine Gipson arrived to the parking lot of Magnolia Gardens, she felt like a weight had been lifted off her. Her husband of thirty-three years had abused her for the last time. She'd put up with Edward's physical and verbal abuse far too long. She replayed the horrific night's events from the night before. Edward had been out drinking with his friends Luther and Mason, their Friday night ritual. Maxine was watching TV when he stumbled in.

"Maxine, where's my dinner?" he yelled from the bedroom.

"It's on the stove," she replied.

"Ain't you gon get it for me?" he stuttered.

"It's still warm. All you have to do is eat it," she replied, changing the channel.

"Woman, when I tell you to do something, you do it." He got close enough to her face, and she could smell the liquor on his hot breath.

"Edward, I—"

"Don't give me any back talk." He yanked her out of the chair and pushed her toward the kitchen.

"You promised you wouldn't put your hands on me again," she cried.

Edward pushed her up against the refrigerator and had her in a chokehold. Maxine gasped for air. She saw her whole life flash by, and at this rate she didn't care if she lived or died.

After a few minutes he let her go and went to the bedroom to watch TV as if nothing happened. Twenty minutes later he was fast asleep.

Maxine stayed up all night thinking about leaving. She'd spent years hiding bruises and black eyes. She'd even stopped going to church because of the embarrassment she felt when one of her friends on the usher board saw a bruise on her arm. Maxine had lied and told her that she burned herself frying chicken. Edward's abuse showed up after he got laid off at the plant he'd worked at for over twenty years. He showed up drunk and had nerve enough to try to drive a forklift. He'd become bitter and angry and with that anger came the abuse. He went from being a once-caring husband to a belligerent bully.

Maxine, at one point, started to blame herself for his behavior, partly because Edward himself always blamed her by saying, "Look what you made me do," or "If you didn't nag me so much I wouldn't be so stressed out." She'd heard them all and now she was fed up. Tired of walking around her own house on eggshells, tired of not knowing if he would be a ticking time bomb and tired of being scared that he would one day kill her. She had planned to leave him before but always felt sorry for him and stayed. This time she'd run for her life and never come back.

The next morning when Edward left for work, Maxine hurriedly packed her clothes and retrieved the mason jar she'd buried with her money in it. Since Edward didn't allow her to work, she saved every dime he gave her, and sometimes she took a few extra dollars when he was sloppy drunk. Months ago she opened an account of her own that he knew nothing about.

When she saw the commercial about Magnolia Gardens several months ago, she envisioned herself living there. Edward would never think to look for her there. Magnolia Gardens was three hours away from Gustrol. With a tank full of gas in her Nissan Maxima that her son purchased for her birthday, she left the only house she'd lived in in her adult life and bid it farewell. Maxine made the three hour trip and let out a sigh of relief. She had never driven that far by herself. The furthest she ever drove was an hour to Bankward to Woolgroves to pick up fabric when she got the urge to sew.

Thank You Lord for allowing me to make it.

Thank You Lord for Your protection.

Lord, give me strength to make it through this process.

Maxine put her shades on, gathered her suitcases, and went inside.

Once inside she rushed to the front desk in hopes that she'd be able to move in today. She didn't have a plan B, but if push came to shove, she'd get a hotel room and figure out her next move.

"Welcome to Magnolia Gardens. How can I help you?" A

fair skinned, freckle faced, plus-sized brunette who looked to be in her forties whose name tag read Brenda greeted her.

"Yes, I-I need somewhere to stay," she said, nervously looking around.

"Okay, here's an application. You can either complete it here or take it with you." Brenda handed Maxine the application.

"I want to move in today," she said in almost a whisper.

"We normally don't do same—"

"I can't go back there. I need to stay here." Maxine choked back her tears.

Brenda came from around the desk and saw that Maxine had two suitcases with her.

"Come with me to my office, Miss... I'm sorry I didn't catch your name."

"Maxine," she said, picking up her suitcase. Brenda carried the other one.

When they stepped inside the office, Maxine removed her shades. Brenda studied her face. She saw her stress lines in her forehead. Her short natural fro was beginning to gray, and her eyes were red and puffy.

"Ms. Maxine, I'm Brenda, and I want to help you as best as I can. Are you in some sort of trouble?"

"No, I'm just tired," she cried.

Brenda handed her some tissues and a bottle of water from her mini fridge. "Did someone hurt you?"

Maxine nodded her head yes.

"Would you like for me to call the police?"

"No, please don't do that. I don't want Edward to know where I am. He'll probably try to kill me." She sobbed.

"Nobody will ever hurt you again." Brenda patted her hand and reassured her.

"Do you have any children or someone you'd like for me to contact?"

"My son is in the military. He's overseas right now." Her son, Phillip, and his wife, Mindy, were due to move back to the states in the next six months, according to the last letter he wrote.

"Alright, let's get your paperwork done, so that I can get you settled in your room."

"Thank you, thank you so much!" Maxine said.

Brenda finished up the paperwork and took the deposit and first month's rent. Maxine had paid her in cash for fear of Edward somehow finding out that she had a bank account. Brenda told her she'd go get a money order for her, since it was against company policy to accept cash as a form of payment.

Maxine followed Brenda down the hallway to her new room.

"You'll be safe here, and you'll make some great friends," Brenda stated.

Maxine simply shook her head. She couldn't wait to get to the room.

"Ms. Brenda, who's that fox you got with you?" Buddy asked when they passed by him.

"Mr. Buddy, mind your business," Brenda replied with a light chuckle.

Maxine ignored him and kept walking.

"I'm trying to get some new business, but you won't let me handle it." He grinned.

"Mr. Buddy thinks he's a lady's man, but don't pay him any attention."

"I won't," Maxine said matter-of-factly. The last thing on her mind was a man.

"Here we are." Brenda unlocked the door, and she and Maxine went inside.

"This brochure tells you where everything is located, this week's activities, and the menu. Feel free to call me if you have any questions." She handed Maxine the brochure.

Maxine took the it and quietly thanked her.

"No worries, everything is going to be alright," she reassured her.

She hugged her and closed the door and double locked it.

When Brenda left, Maxine sat on the couch and released her cry. A cry of freedom, and of hope. She didn't know what she would tell her son. But she wasn't going to worry about that tonight. She was finally free and although her nerves were getting the best of her, she felt she'd made the right decision.

She bowed her head and began to pray.

Lord, I can't thank You enough. I don't know what will come out of this, but I know whatever it is, it'll be for my good. You said in Your word that all things work for our good. That means even what I consider bad will be for my good. Lord, I pray that Edward will get some help with his illness. He is not a bad person. It's that alcohol got him acting crazy. Lord, I just pray for peace, healing, protection and a fresh new start in Jesus name. Amen.

CHAPTER 15

FRENCHETTA HAD WALKED BY THE SMALLER CHAPEL SLOWLY just a few minutes ago. She'd peeked in and seen that the chairs were starting to fill with people. But Zeke hadn't arrived to bible study yet, so she kept on walking past the open doors. There was still ten minutes left before the official start time. With her Bible and notebook in hand, she might be able to casually bump into Zeke, and then they could walk to bible study together. Sit together. *If* she could manage to "accidentally" meet up with him before Norman opened in prayer.

Roaming around looking for a man was so unlike her. So *beneath* her. But truth be told, Zeke was starting to get under her skin. She liked his company. His smile. His words. Even if he did tend to wear the same stained, wrinkled plaid shirt and those cargo pants almost every other day. She had to admit, the clothes didn't stink, so he must have at least been washing them on a regular basis.

"Hey, Frenchie. I see you got your Bible and everything in hand. You heading to bible study?"

The question came from Tracy. Certainly not exactly the person Frenchetta was hoping for.

"As a matter of fact, I am," Frenchetta replied, coming to a halt in the hallway. The intersection of the main hallway and the west hallway was the perfect location to run into Zeke on the way to bible study.

"You got some holy oil in your pocketbook, too?" Tracy laughed.

Frenchetta gave her a smug grin. "No, young lady, I do not. But *you* might want to join us tonight if you don't have anything else to do."

Tracy sighed. "Boredom is my middle name, especially around here." Tracy flailed her arms in the air. "We need, like, a club up in here. You know? With a DJ and a dance floor and drinks. *That's* what we need around here."

"Tracy, we are at *Magnolia Gardens*. Why would you expect a club with a name like that?"

The girl sighed. "I guess you're right. Is anything else going on tonight besides bible study?"

"I wouldn't know. I've been looking forward to this all week. Norman is really a gifted teacher," Frenchetta said.

"He's also fine," Tracy added. "I might join y'all just so I can have a little eye candy tonight. Since we ain't got no margaritas up in here."

"Really, Tracy?"

"Don't judge me. You might be a senior citizen, but you know Norman is hot, too."

Frenchetta engaged Tracy in more small talk, all the while

watching out for Zeke. When the grandfather clock in one of the lounge areas began to chime, Frenchetta decided she'd better go on into bible study without Zeke.

"So, are you coming with us or not?"

"How long is it?"

"About thirty or forty-five minutes. Just depends on how the discussion goes if there are a lot of questions."

"Well, I can stay for about thirty minutes. But I have to go when my show comes on," Tracy said, looking down at her phone.

"Good deal." Frenchetta gently touched Tracy's arm, guiding her toward the small chapel just as the seventh chime sounded.

"Hey! Frenchetta and Tracy! Good to have you both here," Norman greeted them along with the smiles from those already in the room.

"Thank you," Frenchetta said. She and Tracy took their seats.

Norman opened the group in prayer, then passed out notes for the night.

"You didn't tell me we would have homework," Tracy whispered to Frenchetta.

"It's not homework. It's just more information."

"Uuulk," Tracy balked under her breath.

If she weren't so young, Frenchetta might have been annoyed. But at Tracy's age, she probably was young enough to be Frenchetta's own child. Unlike Keith, at least Tracy had enough sense to keep a roof over her head.

Keith had been on Frenchetta's mind a lot lately. He hadn't

called. Wouldn't return her calls. And he'd sounded so desperate the last time she talked to him.

The other day a news report came on about somebody at a nightclub getting shot. Frenchetta had held her breath until she saw a picture of the victim. She didn't wish that kind of pain on any mother, but she breathed a sigh of relief when it wasn't Keith.

This bible study and her increased personal prayer time had done a lot to bring her peace and help her trust God with her son. No matter she and Elroy might have done wrong while raising Keith, she couldn't change the past now. All she could do was place him and her fears and her regrets in the Lord's hands. People used to sing, "He'll work it out." Maybe not when or how we want Him to, but He will.

According to Katrina, Keith was staying with Shayla and hanging out with friends. "Momma, don't worry about him. He's grown. He'll figure it out," Katrina had said.

Still, Frenchetta's feelings hadn't fully processed the memo regarding not worrying about Keith.

"Frenchie?" Norman called her name.

Suddenly, she was aware that this wasn't the first time he'd said her name. Only seconds ago, her ears had heard it, but she hadn't been thinking clearly.

"Yes? I'm sorry. What did you say?"

"Could you please read First John Chapter four, verse nineteen."

Quickly, Frenchetta began flipping through her Bible. "Oh, yes."

Though Tracy didn't seem interested, Frenchetta opened her Bible and laid the right side of it on Tracy's knee while balancing the left side on her own, so they could share the Word. Frenchetta placed a finger on the scripture and said, "I'm reading from the King James Version. We love Him, because He first loved us."

"What does that scriptures mean to you?" he asked.

She thought about it for a moment, then answered, "It means He is very generous with His love. He loves people who don't love Him first. And when we finally get enough sense to see His love, we can't do anything but reciprocate." Even as she spoke the words, the realization of them came to life. *It's hard to love someone who doesn't deserve it ... unless you're God.*

Just then, the door to the chapel opened and in walked Zeke. Frenchetta drunk in his appearance from the floor all the way up. Shined up church shoes, pressed black slacks, a leather belt with a gold clasp, a crisp light blue dress shirt and a striped tie. His hairline and beard were precisely trimmed, framing his face with perfection.

"Mmmmph," Tracy mumbled. "He cleans up quite nicely."

Frenchetta couldn't have agreed more. In fact, she'd had to stop herself from making one of those "mmmmph" sounds like Tracy had. Still, she'd felt a twinge of jealousy when Tracy made that noise.

"Sorry I'm late, everybody. Had a meeting at my old church. They're planning a church reunion," he said, occupying an empty seat behind Lily, nearest the door.

It was all Frenchetta could do to keep her eyes from popping out of her head. *His wife must have been crazy to leave him.*

"No problem, Zeke," Norman said. "Glad you could join us when you did. When's the big event?"

"This coming Sunday. Service, followed by a meal in the fellowship hall." Zeke seemed quite excited.

Will his ex-wife be there? She must have belonged to the church, too. Would she come to the reunion, see Zeke looking like a million bucks, and want him back? Frenchetta was all for saving a marriage, but in this case, she had to admit that she would have been a little sad if that were the case.

Lily chirped, "Sounds like fun. I hope you all have a blessed reunion."

"Thank you." Zeke nodded. "You're all welcome to come." His eyes briefly met up with Frenchetta's, then moved on to Tracy and the others in the room.

"We surely appreciate it," came from someone behind Frenchetta.

Somehow, Frenchetta wasn't too happy about the fact that he'd invited *everyone* with his blanket statement. A personal invitation would have been nice.

Frenchie! Stop it! Zeke is only your friend, nothing more! You're not looking for a man!

"Sorry to interrupt," Zeke apologized again. "Go on with the lesson, please."

"Okay. Frenchie, continue."

"Huh?" Frenchetta asked, dumbfounded.

"Go ahead and finish reading the chapter," Norman directed.

Frenchie glanced down at the Bible. She couldn't remember what verse she'd read last. She could barely remember her name since Zeke walked into the room. "Um ..." her finger ran up and down the page.

Tracy pointed at first John four and twenty. "You're right here."

"Oh. Okay."

Frenchetta managed to read verses twenty and twenty-one, though her voice seemed to tremble.

"Thank you," Norman said before engaging in discussion with the whole group again.

Tracy smiled at Frenchetta. "I see you've got your eye on somebody else these days."

Frenchetta faked shock, whispering, "What?"

"Zeke. I see you two talking here and there. I gotta give it to you. You saw something in him I'm just now seeing tonight," Tracy cooed. "And I usually can spot 'em a mile away."

"Well," Frenchetta warned playfully, "just keep your eyes on your husband."

"Go on, Frenchie. I ain't mad at you." Tracy gave Frenchetta a secret high-five.

CHAPTER 16

MAXINE PACED THE FLOOR, TRYING TO DECIDE WHETHER OR not she would go to the store. A week had passed since she arrived to Magnolia Gardens. She hadn't left the room at all. All of her meals had been delivered, so she felt no need to leave. Brenda had been checking on her and making sure she was okay.

"I think it would do you good if you got out and mingled and made some friends," she'd said on her last visit.

Maxine pondered that idea. She didn't know how to mingle. She really didn't have any friends. The thought of leaving her room made her feel a little uneasy. All sorts of things ran through her mind. What if Edward found her? What if he sent someone to look for her? What if he caught her out by herself and tried to kill her?

She really needed to get out today and purchase a few personal items. She also needed a cell phone. She and Edward had one they shared, and she purposely left it behind. The only numbers she needed were her sister, Cora, and her son and she had both of those memorized. Cora lived in Ohio and they talked twice a month, and she was certain Cora had probably called her. She wanted to contact her before she started worrying about her whereabouts and called the authorities.

Cora would be thrilled to know that she finally got the courage to leave Edward.

One day when Cora had come to visit Edward decided to get flippant with Maxine, but unbeknownst to him, Cora wouldn't back down to him. Standing at five-eight and weighing two hundred seventy-five pounds, she'd placed her hand on her hips and asked, "Who do you think you talking to? I know you ain't talking to my sister." She pointed her finger in his face.

Edward looked Cora up and down but thought better of it. Given his drunken state, she could mop the floor with him.

"Maxine, you deserve better," Cora told her before she left to go back home.

Cora had even tried to get Maxine to move to Ohio with her, but Maxine declined the offer.

Maxine put on a pair of jeans, a light blue sweater and boots, and grabbed her purse and keys. She peeped out the door to make sure she didn't see anyone. She quickly stepped out, locked her door, and turned to walk toward the garage and bumped into someone.

"I'm so sorry," she said.

"It's no problem, Maxine," he said.

With stuttered speech she asked, "How-how do you know my name?"

She took a few steps back, wondering if she should run or not.

"It's okay, I'm Norman a resident director here. I know all of our tenants. I was actually coming to talk to you. Can we step back inside for a few moments?"

"What's this about?" Maxine asked, still nervous, not knowing if it was safe to talk to him or not.

"It won't take long, and I really don't want to discuss this in the hallway," Norman said, flashing her a friendly smile.

Maxine unlocked the door, and Norman followed her inside.

"Have a seat," she offered.

Norman sat on the couch, but she continued to stand with her arms folded.

"Maxine, Brenda told me a little about your situation. So, I wanted to make sure that you are okay and to let you know that we offer counseling services," Norman said, getting right to the point.

"I'm not the crazy one, so why would I need counseling?" Maxine pointed out.

"Maxine, I'm not calling you crazy. You're the victim in all of this. Will you please have a seat so that I can explain to you what type of services we offer?"

Maxine sat on the far end of the couch, and Norman let out a sigh.

"Maxine, abuse can leave psychological wounds that are harder to heal than bodily injuries, which is why we offer counseling. It's on site so you won't have to worry about leaving the facility. I'm sure the transition alone is stressful, and it's a huge scary adjustment," he said, trying to ease Maxine's mind.

It was almost as if Norman was reading her mind. Every night Maxine placed the dining room chair in front of the door, and she had also been having nightmares. As a result of those nightmares, she now slept with the TV on.

"Well, thank you for the information. I'll keep that in mind, Norman," Maxine replied with her head down. She had never thought about talking to anyone about her situation with Edward. It was too embarrassing, and she didn't want anyone in her business.

"We're a family here. We're here to help, and there's no need to feel ashamed. This isn't your fault," Norman reassured her. "You don't have to go through this alone."

"I better get going. I have a lot to do." Maxine stood and waited for Norman to follow suit.

Norman took the hint and stood to leave. "Here's my card. So feel free to call me anytime. And here's a card for the counseling, just in case you want to call them."

"Thank you," she managed to say and took both cards and closed the door behind him.

Maxine's heart was racing, so she took a seat on the couch. Her nerves had gotten the best of her from Norman.

What would I possibly say to a counselor?

Maxine had seen people on TV talking about domestic violence and abuse, but back in her growing up days those terms didn't exist. She witnessed her father fight her mother, and her mother went through life acting as if nothing was wrong.

Maxine remembered one day when they came home from school her father slapped her mother, because her sister Cora had gotten invited to go to the prom. Jimmy Cage, the high school's football quarterback, was Cora's crush, and her mother thought it was a great idea for Cora. But her father wasn't having it. Not only had he slapped her, but he also gave her a black eye.

"No daughter of mine is gon' be courting. She'll mess around and be fast as lightening, and then come up pregnant," her father had said.

Herbert Foley was a drinker and he cursed like a drunken sailor. He whipped his children for every little reason—from talking about boys to not folding the bathroom towels. That's just how she grew up. Her mother, Emma Jean, never complained. Several nights Maxine saw Emma in the den crying and praying, asking God to change Herbert's ways. Maxine asked Emma why wouldn't she just leave.

"I made a vow to Herbert and to the Lord. It won't be like this always," Emma told Maxine.

As the years went by, Herbert's behavior got worse, and the rumor that Maxine and Cora heard from their peers was that he was receiving a crazy check. Herbert later died from diabetes complications. Emma nor the girls knew about his condition because he never went to the doctor. On the day of his funeral, Maxine didn't know if her mother was crying tears of joy or if she really was going to miss him. Both Maxine and Cora were glad to have him out of their lives. *How could you grieve someone who treated you so horribly?* Six months after Herbert's death, Emma died in her sleep. The doctors ruled it as natural causes. Maxine and Cora both felt she died from a broken heart. Emma never had a chance to work, learn to drive, have friends, or experience any of the things that life had to offer.

Maxine blinked back her tears. Those memories were becoming her reality. Edward never allowed her to do too much of anything. The only reason he didn't stop her from driving was because Phillip purchased the car, and Edward always sent her to run his errands. Even then he put her on a time clock. Every now and then she'd risk going to pick up fabric, just to get away. Sewing was the only activity she had in her life that brought her joy. Maxine had become the neighborhood seamstress, but due to Edward's insecurities, he stopped her from doing that, too. Her life had been all about Edward and his needs.

Maxine smoothed her hands on her jeans and looked at the card again. The tears that were threatening to come began to flow like a river.

Maybe I do need to talk to someone. It's time for me to take my life back.

She walked over to her nightstand and picked up the phone receiver. With trembling hands, she dialed the number listed on the card.

CHAPTER 17

THOUGH SHE HADN'T HEARD FROM KEITH IN WEEKS, Frenchetta wasn't going to worry about it. So long as he and Katrina were still talking, that's what mattered. One day he would understand why Frenchetta had to cut him off financially. Until then, she would keep praying for him because, according to Norman and the Bible, God heard prayers even when the subject of those prayers didn't quite want to cooperate.

What neither Norman nor the Bible mentioned, however, was the fact that sometimes God sent something good that you weren't even praying for. Well, on second thought, all those scriptures about Him knowing better than us and about His goodness and mercy should have given her a hint that God had some pretty exciting plans for her up ahead. And it looked as though Zeke was a big part of the plans for her.

Since that night he showed up at the prayer meeting looking quite dapper, Frenchetta began to see him in a new light. Not only did she see *him* differently, she saw *herself* differently. When she first met Zeke, she'd had less-than-ideal thoughts about him because of his style of clothing—or lack thereof. Those wrinkled clothes that didn't even match. She'd wanted to ask him, "Why are you wearing this? Don't you care about how you present yourself to everybody?"

But after being around Zeke, his humor, his easy manner, his plain, basic, truthful conversation, it all made sense now. Zeke liked what he liked and didn't see a reason to switch it up or dress it up, unless there was an occasion like there was when he'd gone to church. Zeke was as comfortable in his wrinkled skin as he was in his wrinkled clothes.

In fact, being around the residents at Magnolia Gardens had turned down a few notches in her judge-o-meter. People did exactly what they wanted to do, and they didn't do things that didn't appeal to them. You could eat breakfast or not. You could play Bingo with a crowd or read a book by yourself. You could have them deliver your lunch to the room or join your friends in the cafeteria. There was no pressure from anybody to do anything you didn't rightfully want to do. And the way Frenchetta saw it, they had all earned that right.

After talking to people here and there, she'd learned that many had served in the military, or as teachers, as housewives, and as business executives who'd successfully followed the rules and regulations all their lives with the dream of one day retiring and doing things their own way. Well, that day was now. Live and let live.

It was quite freeing, actually, to stop spending all her mental energy trying to diagnose everyone's issues, trying to make up a backstory to justify why people like Zeke wore outfits that didn't match with regard to the garments, the jewelry, or even the weather. Frenchetta was getting to a point where she could just look at what they had on and say to herself, "It's not what *I* would wear, but I'm not her and she's not me," and leave it at that.

So when Tracy met Frenchetta in the lobby wearing a velvet, black catsuit with red booties, Frenchetta had to give herself the non-judgmental talk because Tracy was wearing ill-fitting catsuit with unsightly bulges. She didn't quite have the shape to pull off a catsuit, in Frenchetta's opinion. *It's not what I would wear, but I'm not her and she's not me.*

Earnest, however, was grinning ear-to-ear when he met up with Frenchetta and Zeke in the lobby area for their double-date. Earnest had walked down the corridor as though he was walking down the aisle after being pronounced husband and wife with Tracy.

So long as the outfit looks good to him, I guess that's all that matters.

Frenchetta was dressed modestly, in a sleeveless fuschia top with black pants, and a black-and-white shawl. And Zeke, as usual, wore a casual shirt with wrinkled jeans.

The foursome greeted one another with hugs and common clichés.

"We don't want to be late for our bowling time," Earnest said, "so we'd better get going."

One would have thought they were really about to hop into a car and take off, but there was no need for a vehicle. Magnolia Gardens had its own indoor bowling arena, complete with ten lanes and a small pizzeria that was always popping on Saturday nights. Zeke had signed up for an hour and invited Frenchetta. She had, in turn, invited Tracy and Earnest so she could have some more people to, "whip up on," she teased Zeke.

"You really think you're going to beat me bowling?" he had asked when she issued the bold proclamation over a bowl of ice cream for dessert. "Frenchie, you'll probably drop out of the game because you've broken a nail."

Frenchetta raised an eyebrow. "Shows how little you know about me. I was actually in a bowling league. We nearly won state."

"Is that so?"

"You'll find out Saturday night," Frenchetta flirted with a flicker of her lashes.

And now the time had come for her to make good on the promise.

When they all approached the counter to collect shoes, they had no choice except to hear each other's shoe sizes. Frenchetta and Tracy both needed nines. Earnest ordered an eleven. Zeke ordered a thirteen, which caused Tracy to elbow Frenchetta in the ribcage and whisper, "He's got big feet."

Frenchetta quickly pulled herself away from Tracy's sordid humor. "Tracy, really?"

She shrugged. "I'm just sayin'."

Frenchetta shook her head.

"I'll get our lane," Zeke said, and Earnest followed as though men were called to do such things for their women.

Tracy whispered, "Why you actin' all funny? I made one little joke and you're rolling your eyes and acting all bougie."

"I'm not acting funny, and I'm not bougie. It's just... I was raised in an era when ladies didn't talk like that."

"Like what?"

"Like, make innuendos about men's private parts," Frenchetta said with as much tact as possible.

"Okay." Tracy stopped in her tracks and held up a finger. "That's what's wrong with y'all whole generation. Y'all wanted The Cleavers, so y'all made everybody pretend like everything was okay. Everybody wanted to keep up with the Joneses, but nobody knew Mr. Jones was beating Mrs. Jones. Nobody knew Mr. Jones was struggling with depression. Nobody would say anything about the fact that Mrs. Jones' last baby looked like the mailman."

Frenchetta poked her lips out. She thought about being insulted for a moment, but then busted out laughing at the girl's facial expression.

"Shoot, everybody knew that baby was half-white! That's all I'm saying—keep it real!"

"I will admit that we swept a lot of things under the rug in my day. But I still think it's unladylike to discuss some things. Has anyone in your generation ever heard of word discretion? Or wisdom? Or privacy?"

Tracy started walking toward the lanes. "All I know is, we don't keep stuff pinned up inside, and that's a good thing. I mean, if you don't want to joke like I do, fine. I mean, I think it's weird, but I can respect that. All I know is that my momma taught me to speak my mind and don't let anybody try to make you feel like you're wrong for how you feel. And right now, I feel like a size thirteen shoe is good, Frenchie!"

Frenchetta shook her head. "I can't even deal with you right now. But I know one thing, I'm going to clean house with you all tonight in this game."

"Hey now!" Tracy said. "You a good bowler, too?"

"Well, I don't like to toot my own horn but... toot! Toot!" Frenchetta pulled an imaginary handle.

"Yes! I'm pretty good, too. How about we play teams—women against men?"

"You got it!" Frenchetta gave a high-five.

Just as she'd predicted, Frenchetta made a strike on her first bowl and kept the lead the whole time. Tracy hollered out, "That's *my* partner! *My* teammate!" as Frenchetta's score rose higher. "That's *my* homegirl right there!"

Frenchetta couldn't help but boast, too. "Zeke, you got another sport you want to try 'cause bowling surely isn't you at your best, now is it?"

Earnest laughed and slapped Zeke on the back. "She's got a point, doc."

Zeke pushed Earnest's hand away. "Man, whose side are you on?"

Tracy took her turns strutting up to the line in her catsuit. Earnest studied her backside every time. Frenchetta noticed that Zeke turned his head away every time, eating pizza, drinking his drink, tightening his shoelaces—anything to keep from appearing to stare at Tracy's backside.

Frenchetta grew warm inside with appreciation for how Zeke respected Tracy enough not to ogle her. Well, either he respected her or he just didn't want to see all that.

The game was out of reach for the men, thanks to Frenchetta's bowling skills. She and Tracy began singing "Na-na-na-na-hey-hey-hey, goodbye" while there were still two rounds left in the game.

Tracy took it to another level by doing the running-man

dance. That girl danced so hard, lo and behold, she fall flat on her behind.

"Oh my word! Tracy, are you okay?" Frenchetta gasped.

Frenchetta, Earnest, and Zeke rushed to help Tracy get up.

"Baby, are you all right?" Earnest asked.

Tracy moaned. "Oooh wee that hurt."

Zeke asked, "You want us to call an ambulance?"

"No. Let's just...Ooh... I need to sit down for a second."

People from the other alleys came over and inquired about Tracy's well-being, forming a small crowd around her.

"I'm a doctor," one man said.

Frenchetta recognized him as a resident of Magnolia Gardens, but she'd never known he was a doctor. She was always learning new things about her neighbors, even in this scary situation.

The man got down on the floor and shined a light from his cell phone into Tracy's eyes.

"Ow! Get that light out of my eyes! How do we know you even had a license?" Agitated, Tracy used Zeke's and Earnest's arms to lift herself up from the floor.

The doctor announced, "I think she's going to be all right."

Everyone clapped in relief, smiling at Tracy as though she had won an award. Maybe she had won a rare award at Magnolia Gardens—the falling without getting hurt award.

As Tracy sat in the chair at their food table, Frenchetta noticed a big puff of white fabric sticking out of the back of Tracy's catsuit. Her panties were peeking through the hole she must have ripped in her pants when she fell.

"Tracy. Honey, you have to go," Frenchetta said, draping her shawl on Tracy's lap. "Put this around your waist."

Tracy rubbed her hip. "Huh?"

Frenchetta bent down and whispered, "Your pants split open in the back."

Tracy gasped. "Really?"

"Yes. So wrap my shawl around your waist and let's go."

On cue, Tracy quickly wrapped the shawl in place. "Earnest, let's go."

Zeke remained clueless about the split pants until they said goodnight to Tracy and Earnest at the door of their suite.

"Get you some Bengay and get ahead of the pain," Frenchetta told Tracy.

"I ain't got no Bengay," Tracy fussed. "That's for old people."

"Well, you gon' *feel* old in the morning if you don't put it on tonight," Zeke warned.

"I'll give her some of mine," Earnest said as he walked further into their abode.

Frenchetta hugged Tracy goodnight, whispering into her ear, "See. It pays to be with an old man, huh?"

"Bye, Frenchie." Tracy laughed. She took off the shawl and gave it back to Frenchetta. "Thanks."

"Any time."

"Hopefully, there won't be any more times like that."

"Right!" Frenchetta winked at her and said goodnight once again.

Slowly, she and Zeke began walking back to her wing of Magnolia Gardens.

"She took a hard fall," Zeke recalled. "I'm glad she's okay."

Frenchetta replayed that moment in her brain. *One second,*

Tracy was up dancing. The next, she was down on the hardwood floor. "She's young. I think she'll bounce back fine."

The next thing Frenchetta remembered was all the people who had come to help. "Did you see how everyone was, like, right there when she fell?"

"Yeah," Zeke said, looking down at her with confusion. "What else would you have expected? People here care about one another."

"Hmmm," Frenchetta thought out loud. "That's really nice. Like a family."

"For some of the residents, this here is the only family they've got left."

"Wow. I never thought of it that way."

"Yep. This is a real special place, Frenchie. And I'm glad you're here."

"Me, too, Zeke. Me, too."

They walked on to her room and shared a sweet hug before parting ways.

CHAPTER 18

KEITH COULDN'T BELIEVE KATRINA HAD BETRAYED HIM. She'd told him about her visits to Frenchetta and how she felt Frenchetta was the happiest she'd ever seen her. He'd planned to get Katrina to beg Frenchetta to give him some more money to carry him until he got a new job.

"Mama got a new place, haircut, and a new attitude. She's doing her, and frankly I'm happy for her," Katrina had said the last time he spoke to her.

"Forget Mama and Katrina. I don't need them," he mumbled to himself.

"What you say?" Shay sat on the bed next to him.

"Aww nothing."

"I was thinking we could go out tonight after I get off of work. We don't ever go anywhere." Shay snuggled close up to Keith.

"We can't afford to go out. Let me get my money straight

first." Keith got up and went into the closet to search for some clothes.

The truth of the matter was that Keith didn't want to be seen in public with Shay. Shay loved social media and taking selfies, and he couldn't risk his chances of possibly winning Monica back. Monica had a piece of his heart, and if she ever gave him another chance he was going to make things right.

"You always say that," Shay whined.

"Look, Shay, you can't be nagging me about going out. I'm here with you every day, every night, spending time with you," he said, putting on a black t-shirt and a pair of jeans.

"Yeah, you are. But I wanna go out with my man sometimes, unless you are secretly seeing somebody else." She got off the bed and stood in his face.

"There you go with that nonsense. How could I possibly be seeing somebody else when I'm always with you?"

"You're not always with me. You have the car every day while I'm at work. I don't know what you're doing." Shay's voice was shaky.

"Shay, you know you're my girl." Keith wrapped an arm around her shoulders and pulled her close, gently rubbing her arm. "You have nothing to worry about," he assured her.

Shay hugged him tighter and planted a kiss on his lips. She tried to get him to take the kiss deeper, but Keith pulled away. "What was that about?"

"What was what about? Why you tripping, Shay?" Keith was irritated.

"Why didn't you want to kiss me?"

"I did kiss you, Shay. I'm trying to hurry up so that I can meet Raboone. He got a gig for me to make some money."

"On a Sunday. What kind of gig?" Shay questioned him. "And what kinda name is Raboone?"

"His name is Robert Boone, but everybody just call him Raboone. He's going to tell me all about it when I get there. But you holding me up. I mean I can sit here and talk to you all day if you want me to... Or I can go make some money so that we can go out." Keith sat back on the bed and waited for her reply.

"Go ahead and go with Raboone, but don't stay gone too long. I wanna take Justin to get a new pair of shoes. When you come back, maybe we can go to dinner."

"Yeah, maybe so." Keith got the keys off of the dresser and headed toward the door.

Shay was right behind him."Ummm aren't you forgetting something?" She puckered up her lips for another kiss.

Keith forced a smile and kissed her. Shay let out a little whimper, letting him know she wanted more.

Man I gotta hurry up and get up outta here. This girl driving me crazy.

He weighed his options, and decided to go with it to keep her happy, so that he could use the car.

"Alright, baby, have a good day. Can't wait for you to get back home so we can continue this." Shay smacked her lips.

"Okay cool, I'll be back." Keith left before she could say anything else to him.

❦

KEITH DROVE TO THE SOUTH SIDE OF TOWN TO MEET UP with his childhood friend, Raboone. He had told Keith that he needed help with his business and that he would pay him cash for helping out. Keith pulled up in front of Nip's Liquor and Wine just as Raboone had told him via text. He spotted him talking on the phone, so he blew the horn to get his attention. Raboone signaled Keith to give him a minute to wrap up his call.

Raboone wore a hoodie, a pair of jeans, and his mouth was full of gold.

"Say, man, long time no see," Raboone said after he got into the car.

"I know, man, you still look the same. Where are we going?" Keith asked.

"Go by my brother, Lonnie, house, so we can pick up the stuff. I ran into a little car problem, so we'll need to use your car. If that's okay."

"Okay, so what exactly are we doing?" Keith eyed him.

"Selling sheets and comforter sets."

"Man, where you get the stuff from? It ain't hot, is it?" Keith quizzed him.

"Calm down, it's all good. You scared?"

"Naw, let's go," Keith said, feeling a little uneasy.

Keith drove the two blocks and turned into Lonnie's driveway.

"I'll be right back," Raboone said and went to the back of the house.

After about ten minutes he returned with two big trash bags. "Pop the trunk," he instructed Keith.

Keith popped the trunk to Shay's black Ford Escape and waited for Raboone to get in.

"Alright, let's roll. We going to Germica's Beauty Shop. That's where we'll set up."

"Do you need to get permission from the owner?"

"Man, naw. I got this. This ain't my first time doing this. Don't worry about the details," Raboone said with agitation in his voice.

When they arrived at the beauty shop, Raboone told Keith that they would alternate standing outside, since it was so cold. The basic comforter sets were fifty dollars, the comforters with team logos were seventy-five dollars, and the sheets were twenty dollars no matter the size for both.

After about an hour or so Keith got the hang of things and even convinced a few people who wanted just sheets to get a comforter. The ladies coming out of the beauty shop almost bought them out. He and Raboone were both cold and got back inside of the truck.

"Ohh wee, man, the hawk is out." Raboone rubbed his hands together, trying to keep warm.

"Yeah, man, it's probably time to call it quits. Besides I gotta get going." Keith started the truck.

"I got a text from somebody wanting ten sets of sheets. They on they way, so let's make this two hundred dollars and then we can bounce."

"Here's your pay for today." Raboone handed Keith five hundred dollars.

Keith's eyes lit up like a Christmas tree. "Thanks, man. Good lookin' out. Hopefully I'll get squared away soon." Keith took the money and put it in his wallet.

"No problem, there's more from where that came from." Raboone flashed him a smile.

Keith looked in the rearview mirror and saw three cops' cars pulling up behind them, blocking them in.

"Man, if they ask you any questions, play dumb," Raboone said.

"Ask me what? I thought you said this was legit," Keith fussed.

Two more cop cars surrounded them and told them to get out of the car. Raboone tried to run, but one of the cops tripped him and made him fall. The officer then handcuffed him and shoved him against the car.

"Officer, why are we being detained?" Keith nervously asked.

"So you really wanna play dumb, huh?" asked the officer whose badge read Williams.

"I guess he thought he could get away with selling stolen merchandise," his partner Jenkins chimed in.

"Stolen Man you said...." Keith shook his head in disbelief and looked at Raboone, who was looking lost.

Jenkins placed the cuffs on Keith, and the officers put both Keith and Raboone in the back of the squad car.

Keith was more upset with himself than he was with Raboone. He assumed that since Raboone had been to jail more than a few times, he was now on the straight and narrow. A part of him felt like what they were doing couldn't possibly be right. But what choice did he have? He needed the money. Shay was going to be mad about her car, but all he could do was pray that they didn't tow it since it was in front of the beauty shop and not on the street. He knew Shay didn't have the money to get him out, and—as bad as he hated it—he would have no choice but to call Frenchetta.

CHAPTER 19

Frenchetta didn't recognize the number coming through on her cell phone. She was inclined not to answer, but since it was so late in the evening—too late for solicitors to be calling—she went ahead and tapped the green button to accept the call.

"Hello?"

"You have a collect call from..." the automated voice said.

There was a pause, then she heard, "Keith Davenport," from her own son. There was another pause.

Frenchetta pursed her lips. *Why on earth is this boy calling me collect?* In fact, Frenchetta didn't even think there was such a thing as a collect call anymore.

But the next words from the automated announcer cleared up the confusion. "This person is an inmate in the Orchid Falls County jail."

"What!" Frenchetta yelled at the voice. *Jail? My Keih? In jail?* This must be a case of mistaken identity.

"Press one to accept all charges. Press two or simply hang up to decline."

Of course, she would press one to find out what had happened to Keith. Her next call would probably be to a lawyer, she thought. She just needed to hear from her son what had gone wrong. With the strained relationships between black men and police, surely he had been unfairly profiled.

After the phone system gave notification that the conversation might be recorded and processed her permission, Frenchetta heard Keith's voice loud and clear.

"Momma! Thank you!"

Frenchetta was relieved that her son sounded coherent. Healthy. And his speech was clear, so he still had all his teeth. Those officers hadn't beat him senseless after they falsely arrested him.

"You're welcome, Keith. Now, what happened? Are you all right? Did they pull you over for no reason?"

"No, ma. I ... I'm gonna need your help to get out."

"Wait, but what happened?" Frenchetta asked again.

"I can't make any statements right now. I don't want to incriminate myself. What I need from you is to come get me out."

Frenchetta tried another angle. "What are you charged with?"

"They said somethin' like possession of property and, like, boosting. But they ain't got no proof of nothin'," Keith said.

Frenchetta's heart sank. She knew her son. His tone, his word choice, and the fact that Keith was banking on the idea that there was no proof let her know that this was no case of police dragging an innocent man to jail. No, they had arrested a guilty man, clear as day.

"So I'mma need a few thousand to make bail. My homeboy who got arrested with me, Raboone, said it won't be that much because we wasn't doin' nothin' but standing by the sheets and comforters."

"Sheets and comforters?" Frenchetta asked, her head still swimming with the awful truth. "What do bed linens have to do with this?"

"That's what they tryna say, that me and Raboone was selling 'em outside a beauty shop."

"That makes no sense!"

"Right!" Keith agreed. "I mean, we just happened to be standing next to a table, and—"

"No!" Frenchetta yelled. "What doesn't make sense is why you would be starting your life of crime by selling bed sheets!"

"Momma, I'm not in a life of crime. Come on now."

"Well, were y'all selling the stuff or what?" Frenchetta demanded.

"Momma, I already told you I can't talk on this phone."

"Keith, you don't have to say another word. I already know the truth."

"Good. I'm glad we're on the same page because this whole situation is crazy. I mean, we got hardened criminals on the street jacking cars and murdering people, and they arrest me for something this silly?"

Frenchetta's mouth was wide open. Her son's reasoning was so far away from reality, it scared her. It was bad enough he was lying to her, but he was also lying to himself about the severity of his situation.

"I can't wait to get out of jail. So, I say give it another hour or so, then come on up here and get me. You straight?"

The air escaped her lungs in spasms. "Keith. I don't know what to say."

"Say you're on your way."

"No. I will not come get you out of jail, Keith Anthony Davenport. You're in jail, and rightfully so. I am not going to run all over creation trying to free the Bedsheet Bandit. If you don't care enough about your life to stop living so raggedy, why should I?"

"Umm... because you're my mother and—"

"This phone call will end in two minutes," the automated voice announced, breaking up their conversation.

"... for all my life," Keith finished up his thoughts, most of which Frenchetta hadn't heard. Not that it mattered. Keith's train of thought had lost its toot-toot here recently.

"Son, I love you. I always have and I always will. But this lifestyle you're leading... I can't. I'll go broke trying to support both me and you, with all your emergencies. It's as though you live from crisis to crisis, Keith. You need help."

"Maybe I'll get help when you get me out of here," he tried. "So will you do it, Momma?"

Frenchetta sat on the foot of her bed, pondering his question while the cell phone was still warm against her cheek. She had the money to get him out. And she had been willing to pay for a lawyer. But that was before she realized her son was on the wrong side of the law.

Elroy would have been so disappointed in this moment. Thoughts of her husband caused tears to rush to her eyes. One thing Elroy had always told the kids was that if they ever got themselves in trouble with the law, he would let them spend twenty-four hours in jail before he made a move to get them out. *"That'll give you something to think about and keep you from going back there again."* Thankfully, Elroy had never had to enforce that rule.

"One minute," the automated voice came from the phone.

"Momma, we only have a minute. Are you coming to get me out?"

"What time did you go to jail?"

"I don't know. I guess around three o'clock, maybe? It's not like I was looking at the clock when the door slammed."

Frenchetta balled her left fist and set it firmly on her knee. Somehow that move brought strength.

"Keith. I'm going to do what your daddy always said he would do. I'm not coming up there until three o'clock tomorrow. That'll mark twenty-four hours."

"Mom, are you kidding me?"

"No."

"Really? I'm sitting in a jail while you're in your fancy old folks' home, spending up all that money Daddy made. I mean, did you really love him anyway? Or were you just a gold-digger, 'cause I really can't tell right now. You're acting so—"

The call ended abruptly, just as they had been warned. She was thankful for the relief.

Frenchetta set the phone on the bed as tears streamed down her cheeks. Keith's accusation stung deep down inside. He had turned on her in the worst way. *Am I a failure as a mother? I must be, otherwise, how could my son do this to me?*

Maybe she should have just rushed down to the jail. Maybe she should never have moved into Magnolia Gardens. Then

Keith would have had a place to stay, and he wouldn't be out on the streets selling sheets.

Frenchetta's heart was beating with so much sorrow, she could feel it aching, physically. Before long, her body heaved with her crying. Her shoulders bounced up and down as she broke from the inside out.

"Where did we go wrong? Why does Keith hate me?" she asked of herself between sobs.

Suddenly, something Norman had said in one of their meetings popped into her memory. She had put a sticky note on a particular scripture. Frenchetta rushed over to her nightstand and retrieved her purple Bible. She quickly found the lime green marker and flipped to James Chapter five. She had highlighted the first part of the verse: *Is anyone among you in trouble? Let them pray.*

This Scripture was definitely describing her. She was definitely in trouble with regard to Keith. Because even though everything other than Keith was going well in her life, she was experiencing the adage: A mother is only as happy as her least happy child.

The Scripture, however, was giving her hope. Right there, in black and white, in a book she'd been around all of her life but never really opened much, was the answer to what she should do every time she was in trouble. Pray.

Which is exactly what Frenchetta did. It wasn't one of those pretty say-your-grace prayers, either. Frenchetta melted onto the carpeted area of her living area floor and simply stretched out, laid down on her stomach, and cried out to the Lord. "God, You know. You know Elroy and I did the best we knew how to do at the time. I'm so sorry we didn't come to

You more. Maybe things would have been different, maybe not. I don't know, Lord, but I know You do. Oh, God, please don't let anybody hurt my son while he's in jail. Please, Lord, have mercy on him."

Frenchetta went on crying and praying, pleading for Keith, pouring out her heart to God about everything from being mad at Him for Elroy's death to thanking Him for bringing Katrina and the grandchildren back into her life.

She talked to Him as though she were talking to her best friend.

And by the time she finished, she felt like He was.

CHAPTER 20

MAXINE WAS STARTING TO FEEL A LITTLE BETTER ABOUT HER stay at Magnolia Gardens. Her counselor had been great with helping her sort through her feelings and Maxine had even started to get out of her room a little more. Today would be her first time attending an actual event and although she was a little nervous, she was somewhat excited. The brochure stated that they would teach a class on how to make a fleece blanket without actually sewing. Maxine was old school, she made all of her blankets and quilts the old-fashioned way. She couldn't wait to see what the young people had come up with.

When Maxine arrived to the room, she took a seat at the first table she saw available. Two others were at the table.

"Hello, I'm Lily and this is Frenchie. We're your neighbors."

"Hi, I'm Maxine."

"So, where are you from?" Frenchetta asked, trying to make conversation.

"I'm not from around here," Maxine said, not really wanting to give them too much information.

"Why don't we ever see you? You barely come out of your room," Lily said bluntly.

Frenchetta side-eyed her to let her know to cut it out.

"What she means is that you've been here for a while and we never see you." Frenchetta tried to clean it up.

"Yeah, that's what I meant." Lily smiled.

"Alright ladies, I'm Amber. I'll be your instructor today. Let's get started on our blankets. There's fabric for you to choose from over here," she stated.

Maxine was glad that she'd come in to start the class. She wasn't in the mood to answer any more questions. She quickly got up from her chair to retrieve her fabric.

Frenchetta and Lily joined her in search of their fabric as well.

"Great minds think alike," Frenchetta said as she and Maxine ended up with the same colors: black, green and white.

Lily, on the other hand, had orange, blue, and brown.

"I guess so." Maxine smiled.

"You'll be working with the people at your table. We're taking things step-by-step, so don't be afraid to stop me if I'm going too fast or if you have questions."

The ladies worked in silence and for the most part they were able to follow Amber's directions, that is, until Frenchetta had trouble trying to cut her corners.

"Now how in the world am I supposed to know how much a five inch square is?" Frenchetta asked. "I don't want my blanket to look a mess."

"I think my blanket may be a little lopsided." Lily giggled.

"We can measure by this cardboard that says five inch." Maxine held up the piece of cardboard she'd gotten from the basket on the table. She was almost done cutting her four corners.

"Can you do mine, too?" Lily asked.

"Sure, let me show you." Maxine gathered the fabric and cut Lily's four corners perfect.

"You look like you know what you're doing." Frenchetta pointed out.

"I used to sew," Maxine replied.

"By now you should be ready to cut your fringes on all four sides of the blanket. Cut through both layers of fabric at the same time. The fringe pieces should be a little wider than the width of your finger. Cut in from the edge five inches," Amber instructed.

Both Lily and Frenchetta looked at one another in total confusion. Maxine had already started cutting hers.

"Maxine, you're going to have to show me how to do mine," Frenchetta said.

"Yeah, me too," Lily chimed in.

Maxine finished up her blanket and showed Frenchetta and Lily how to cut the fringes. Once they got the hang of things, they all started the final step which was to tie the fringes into balloon knots.

"I don't know if ole Arthur will let me tie all of these knots," Frenchetta said.

"Who is Arthur?" Lily asked, looking around.

Both Frenchetta and Maxine burst out laughing.

"What's so funny?" Lily asked.

"Arthur is short for arthritis," Frenchetta informed her.

"Oh okay, now I get it." Lily snickered.

Maxine laughed. She couldn't remember the last time she actually laughed. It felt good to be around people who seemed to be so nice.

"This is actually really neat," Frenchetta said as she and Maxine finished up her blanket.

"I didn't know how this would turn out without a sewing machine, "Maxine said, holding up her blanket.

"I was thinking the same thing," Lily stated.

"I'm glad I let you talk me into coming, Lily." Frenchetta smiled.

"It was a lot of fun, and we got a chance to make a new friend," Lily replied.

"I'm glad I came, too. Thanks for showing yourselves friendly toward me. I really enjoyed myself," Maxine said.

"We'll have to hang out again soon," Frenchetta said.

"I'd like that," Maxine stated.

"You can be a part of the Golden Girls part 2." Lily giggled.

Maxine looked to Frenchetta for an explanation.

"I'll fill you in on that later. Let's go get some lunch. Lily, are you coming?"

"I'm kinda tired. I think I'll take a nap before the *T.J. Hooker* marathon comes on. You ladies have fun." Lily grabbed her belongings and left the room.

"Let's go drop these blankets off first, so they won't get dirty," Frenchetta suggested.

"Okay, sounds like a plan." Maxine followed Frenchetta out the door, towards the lobby. She had a little more pep in her step, and for the first time in a long time she actually felt good.

"I hope they have those Mexican chicken wraps. They are so good," Frenchetta said.

When Maxine didn't answer, Frenchetta turned to see what was going on. Maxine had stopped dead in her tracks.

"What's wrong? What is it?" Frenchetta asked.

A man dressed in all black was ranting and raving and walking fast towards them.

Maxine appeared to be horrified.

"It's Edward, my husband," she said in almost a whisper.

"I knew I would find you. What made you think you could just leave me?" Edward grabbed Maxine by her arm and twisted it behind her back.

Tears began to stream down her face. "Leave me alone...." she said, trying to get loose.

"Help, help! Somebody help us!" Frenchetta screamed.

"Got me worried and looking a fool, trying to find you." He pushed Maxine toward the door. Frenchetta tried to break them apart and he pushed her, causing her to stumble.

Buddy and Zeke came running up the hall to aid them.

"Frenchie, are you alright?" Zeke asked.

Frenchetta nodded her head.

"Man if you don't get your hands off of her," Zeke pushed Edward off of Maxine.

"You can't tell me what to do with my own wife," he said with slurred speech. His breath reeked of liquor.

"Maxine, are you okay?" Frenchetta rushed to her side.

"That's him. That's the guy who rammed his truck through the gate," the security officer said, running towards them with

Norman right behind him. The security team apprehended Edward.

"The police are on the way," Norman instructed them.

"Maxine, baby, tell them everything is alright," Edward begged.

"No, everything is not alright," she cried.

Lily ran down the hallway frazzled. "Guys, what's all the commotion?"

"Everything's under control now," Buddy assured her.

Moments later the police arrived and arrested Edward.

"Maxine, you gon' miss me. You gon' regret this. It ain't over til I say it's over," Edward yelled as they took him out of the building.

"It's okay, you're safe now." Frenchetta hugged her.

"Yeah, he won't be bothering you ever again," Zeke said.

"I'll make sure of it," Buddy added.

"And I will, too," Norman said.

Frenchetta, Norman, Zeke, Lily and Buddy followed Maxine to her room to make sure she got settled in.

Frenchie, Lily, and Maxine sat on the couch, and the guys pulled chairs from the dining table.

"Frenchie and I will stay with you tonight if you'd like, won't we Frenchie?" Lily offered.

"We sure will." Frenchetta smiled and patted her hand.

Maxine shook her head yes, giving her approval.

"Thanks for being here with me. You don't really know me, but yet you're here," she managed to say.

"You don't have to thank us. We're all family," Norman said.

Frenchetta couldn't help but tear up a little. Norman was

right. They were all family. That's what they had all been to her since her arrival. Even Buddy, in his own annoying way. This was confirmation that she'd made the right choice after all by taking a step of faith in a new direction. She was sure the best was yet to come.

ALSO BY CASANDRA & MICHELLE

If you enjoyed this book by CaSandra and Michelle,
be sure to read Deacon Brown's Daughters.

Here's the First Chapter

Chapter 1

He was used to getting messages from random women. These days, the messages usually came through his phone in the form of a text or an email. Whoever wrote this one must have had a lot on her mind because she had taken the time and effort to write neat, cursive letters on the front and use an oversized envelope.

It was addressed To: Stanley David Brown, Care of: Effie Brown, followed by his mother's address in Big Oak, TX.

Stanley chuckled to himself as he laid the envelope on his nightstand. Whatever this blast from the past had to say to him would have to wait until he got out of his work clothes and had a glass of Jack Daniels to warm up.

No. Not Jack Daniels. He had to remind himself that he was a changed man. Even a whole year after accepting Christ, his mind returned to its old default ways without conscious resistance. Though Stanley had never been an alcoholic, he recognized alco- hol as a gateway to the past for him. No need in going back there.

Besides, it was two in the afternoon. Saturday overtime was

always finished before he knew it. Coffee was still in order.

"Stan-laaaaay!"

He ignored his mother. She would call at least three more times before adding his middle and last name.

Stanley slid his aching feet from the steel-toed boots he'd purchased for his new job as a forklift operator. The position was well below his intelligence, but probably right in line with what his work history was worth. He was one of the oldest men working in that position at Transit Systems Deluxe. Most of the men his age didn't work the dock. They were truck drivers, dispatchers, supervisors. Too old to be outside in the cold trying to coerce 52-year-old bones to keep pushing.

The tender spots on his feet welcomed the soft carpet as he walked down the short hall between his current bedroom and the bathroom.

"Stan-laaaaay!"

That was only twice. He knew he should respond to her, but he also knew what she wanted, and he couldn't give her an answer yet to who had written him a letter and mailed it without a return address. Out of respect, he yelled, "Wait a minute, Momma," as he shut the door behind him.

The two-story home had been one of the most well-kept homes on their street when he was a little boy. But his mother had refused to update the house. She replaced things as they were needed, but hadn't put any real effort into replacing the linoleum tile or removing the flowered wallpaper. "Keeps the character," she had said.

Now that Stanley was home, he'd offered to at least paint over the wallpaper. He'd seen it done once on a do-it-yourself show.

"Naw, leave it be. It'll be back in style in a little while," Effie

refused.

If somebody had told Stanley a year ago, before he went to that Sunday morning service at Lee Chapel, that he'd be moving back home to take care of his mother, he would have told them they'd been drinking too much.

Stanley ran his hand along his chin. He could have used a good shave. He'd have to shave, actually, before Sunday night. Part of the work dress code.

He turned his head to the left. To the right. Admiring his pro- file in the bathroom mirror. He smiled at his reflection—smooth, deep-brown skin, white teeth, a broad nose, and grayish-green eyes that caused even the most modest woman to do a double-take. At which point, he always blinked and flashed all 32. That's all it took, for the most part. Then came a date or two. Maybe three if his game wasn't slippin'. Then came the bedroom and she'd be all his after that.

If he couldn't get anything else, he could always get a woman. And with a woman came food, a place to stay, and electricity. That's all he'd ever needed to survive.

Until Jesus.

He straightened up tall and stuck his chest out, still admiring his 6'4" frame. Those guys on the dock might have been younger and faster, but none of them would look half as good as him at his age.

Stanley turned on the shower to let the water warm up.

An old house like this still needed time to do what it was sup- posed to do. Kind of like his feet and back, which had not yet decided that they were on the work-six-days-a-week plan.

"Stanley David Brown!" Time was up.

Stanley briskly walked to the kitchen and stood over his mother. This woman right here could work his nerves something fierce. "Momma, stop hollering my name. I'm right in the next room."

"You actin' like you can't hear me, though!" She folded her newspaper and looked up at him over the rim of her glasses. Stan- ley saw the gray ring around her eyes, the wrinkles circling her neck, even the knobs on her knuckles from arthritis. His sister, Emily, had been right. Momma couldn't have moved to Detroit with them for Emily's husband's new job. The trip would have taken a toll on her body, not to mention the fit she would have thrown about leaving her house.

In an instant, Stanley was thankful to have been in a position to step in where Emily had to leave off.

Effie motioned toward Stanley's bedroom. "Who that letter from?"

"I don't know yet." "One of your women?"

"I don't have any women."

"Hmph. That's a first."

Stanley shook his head. "I'm going to take a shower now." "Well, bring the letter to me. I'll open it."

"No can do. It's addressed to me. If you open it, that's a felony."

"Felony my foot. Long as you stayin' under my roof, I got

rights! I shoulda opened it already, anyway, since it came to my care. Now, come on and open it else I'll sneak in there and open it while you in the shower."

Stanley laughed. "If you tell me you're going to sneak, that's not actually sneaking, now is it?"

Effie slapped his arm. "You stop it. Go on. Turn off that

shower water and come back in here." "I don't smell good," Stanley teased.

"You smell like a hard-working man, and that's the best smell ever. Now, stop playin' with me and get the letter before you make me have a heart attack from worryin'."

Drama.

Stanley dutifully obeyed. He turned off the water, grabbed the letter, and joined his mother at the kitchen table again. The table wobbled a bit, which meant the folded up paper he'd put under the short leg must have wiggled itself loose. Stanley reached down and tucked the paper back in place again. His mother wouldn't dream of letting this table go.

"This is the highlight of your day, huh?" He sulked, tearing the back flap off the envelope while looking into his mother's bucked eyes.

"Might be a late Christmas present. It's only been a week or so."

"Could be," Stanley agreed, though he doubted it. This was probably some woman from his past who wanted to let him know how he'd ruined her life, her credit, her trust in men or in all of hu- manity. He'd heard it all before: *I thought you were the one! You deserve an Emmy award for your acting skills!*

Truth be told: There was nothing a woman could say to him that he hadn't already beaten himself up about, especially in the past year as he had begun to realize his new identity. He almost wished he could round them all up on a football field, get a bull- horn, and announce to them, "I am sorry. I wish I could change the past, but I can't. I apologize for whatever I might have done to hurt you. Y'all can go on home now."

And then, of course, he would take off running. "Oh no!" His mother gasped.

Stanley's attention turned to the contents now. He pulled out a folded program. The front of it had a bright yellow sticky note: *F.Y.I.*

He removed the note and came face to face with the picture of a young man who was the spitting image of the face he'd just been adoring in the mirror.

Stanley's heart felt like a stone rock in his chest.

"What is it?" Effie asked.

"An obituary."

Effie's hand covered her neck. "Who?"

"My son."

ABOUT THE AUTHORS

CaSandra McLaughlin was raised in Marshall, Texas. Growing up she wrote poems and loved to read books. She remembers be- ing excited every time the book mobile came to her school. Read- ing always took her to another place, and often she would find herself rewriting an author's story. CaSandra wrote a play in high school for theatre that she received a superior rating on, and from there she aspired to be a writer.

CaSandra's a true believer that God has blessed us all with gifts and talents and it's up to us to tap into them to make our dreams come true. She's always dreamed of being on radio, TV and being an author. CaSandra currently works for a Gospel radio station and now she's an author. That lets her know that dreams come true—two down and one more to go. CaSandra wants peo- ple to read her work and feel encouraged, and it's her prayer that they read something that will change their lives and give them a ray of hope that things will be better. She's praying that God will continue to use her to write novels with several life lessons to help inspire the world.

CaSandra currently lives in Glenn Heights, Texas with her husband Richard and they have two amazing children.

CaSandra loves God, her family, church, her friends, reading and Mexican food, in that order. Peace and blessings to all. Thanks for the love and support.

Visit CaSandra McLaughlin Online at
www.CaSandraMcLaughlin.com
http://www.facebook.com/casandra.marshallmclaughlin

Michelle Stimpson's works include the highly acclaimed *Boaz Brown*, *Divas of Damascus Road* (National Bestseller), and *Falling Into Grace,* which has been optioned for a movie. She has published sev- eral short stories for high school students through her educational publishing company at WeGottaRead.com.

Michelle serves in women's ministry at her home church, Oak Cliff Bible Fellowship. She regularly speaks at special events and writing workshops sponsored by churches, schools, book clubs, and educational organizations.

The Stimpsons are proud parents of two young adults, grand- parents of one super-sweet granddaughter, and the owners of one Cocker Spaniel, Mimi, who loves to watch televangelists.

Visit Michelle online:
www.MichelleStimpson.com
https://www.facebook.com/MichelleStimpsonWrites